DERIB + JOB

YAKARI

AND GREAT EAGLE

9th CINEBOOK
The 9th Art Publisher

Original title: "Yakari et le grand aigle"

Original edition: © Le Lombard (Dargaud-Lombard S.A.) 1973, by DERIB + JOB
www.lelombard.com

English translation: © 2005 Cinebook Ltd

Translator: Erica Jeffrey
Lettering and text layout: Imadjinn sarl

This edition first published in Great Britain in 2005 by
CINEBOOK Ltd
56 Beech Avenue
Canterbury, Kent
CT4 7TA
www.cinebook.com

Second printing: March 2009
Printed in Spain by Just Colour Graphic

A CIP catalogue record for this book
is available from the British Library

ISBN: 978-1-905460-04-5

9th CINEBOOK
The 9th Art Publisher

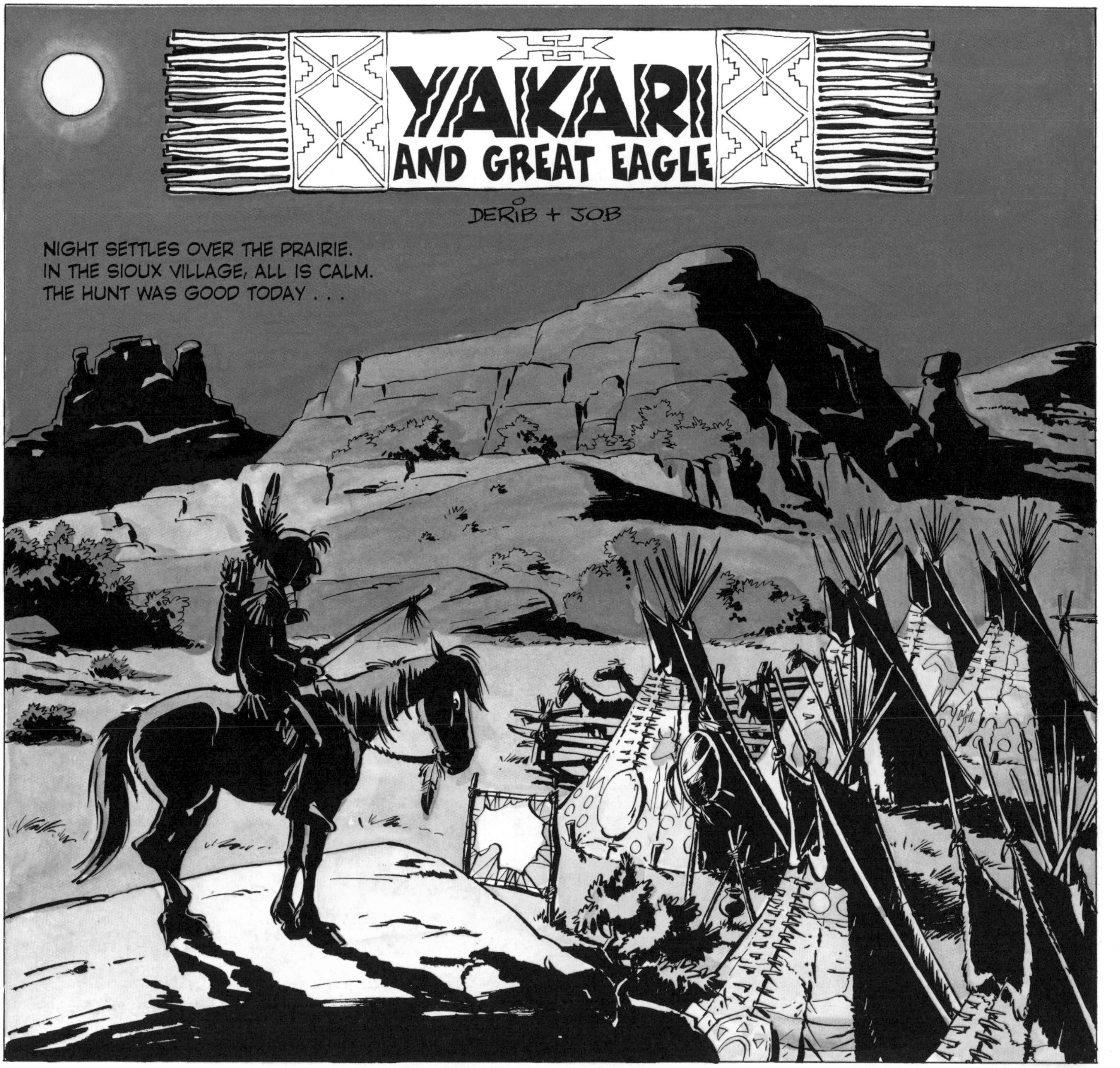
YAKARI
AND GREAT EAGLE
DERIB + JOB
NIGHT SETTLES OVER THE PRAIRIE.
IN THE SIOUX VILLAGE, ALL IS CALM.
THE HUNT WAS GOOD TODAY . . .

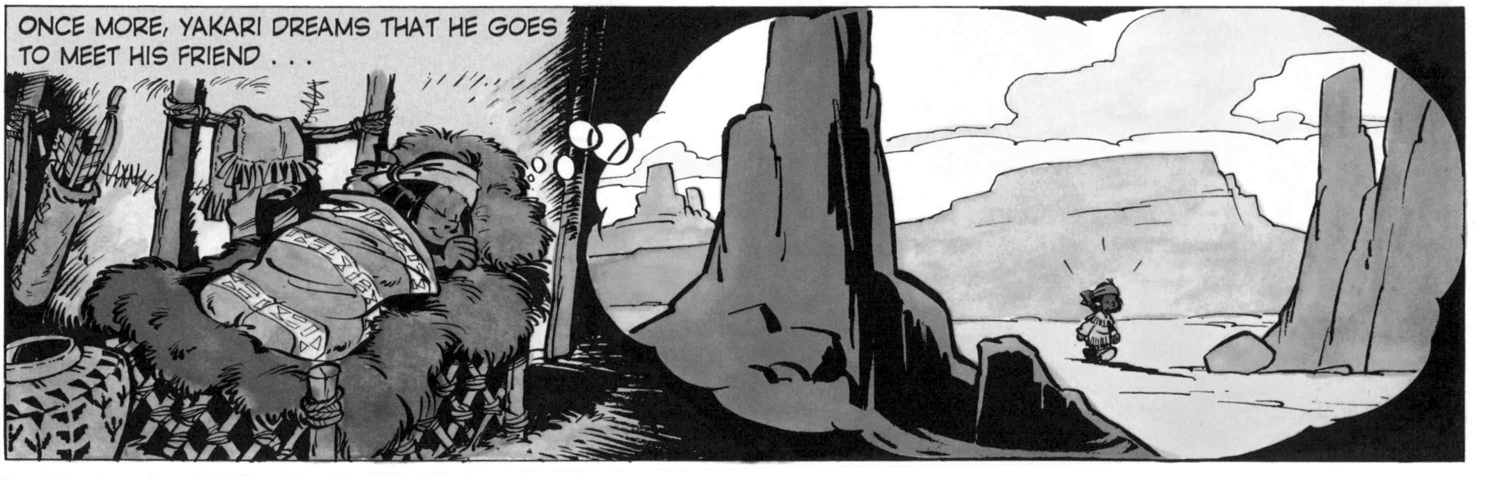
ONCE MORE, YAKARI DREAMS THAT HE GOES
TO MEET HIS FRIEND . . .

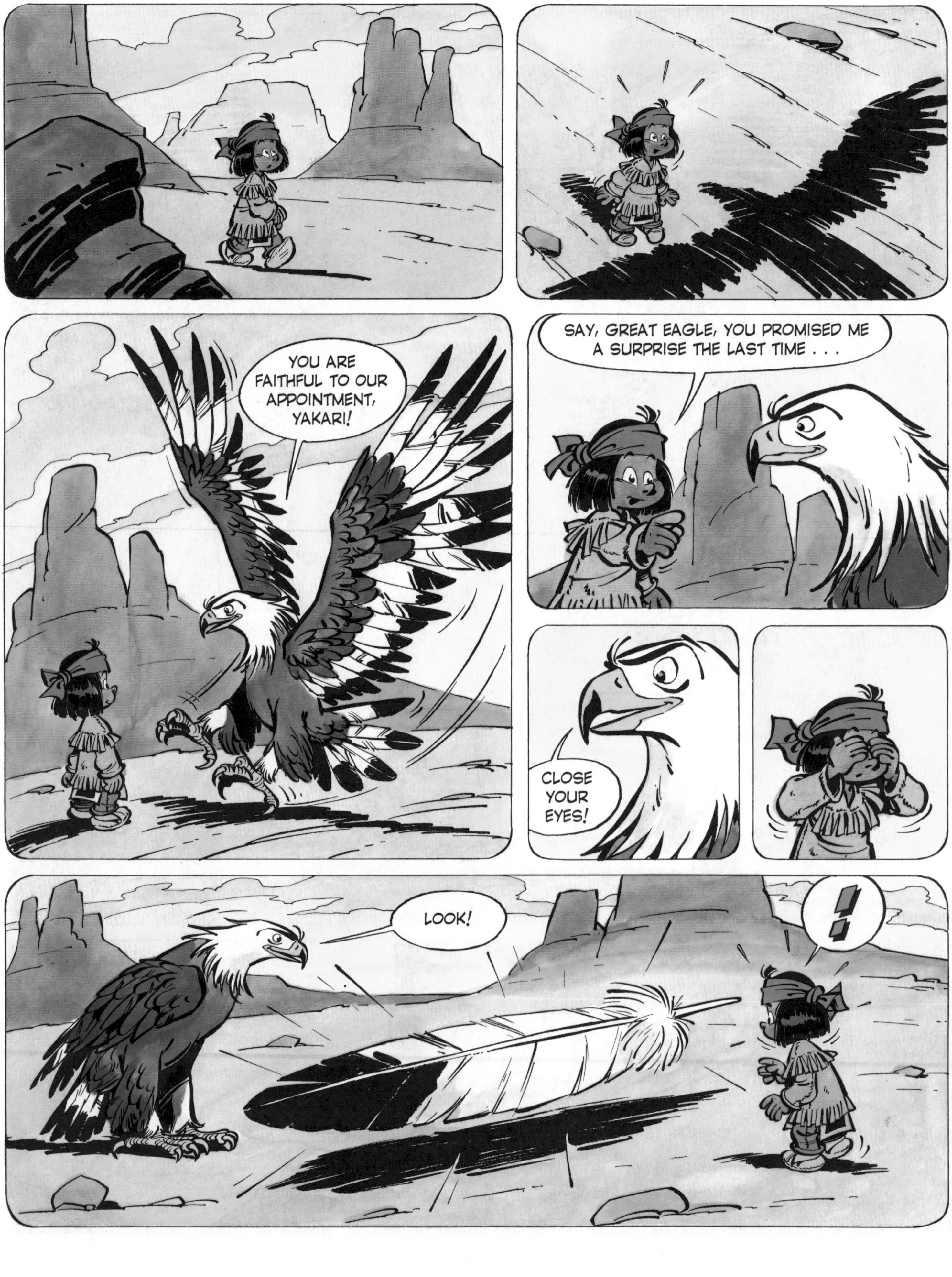
YOU ARE FAITHFUL TO OUR APPOINTMENT, YAKARI!
SAY, GREAT EAGLE, YOU PROMISED ME A SURPRISE THE LAST TIME . . .
CLOSE YOUR EYES!
LOOK!
!

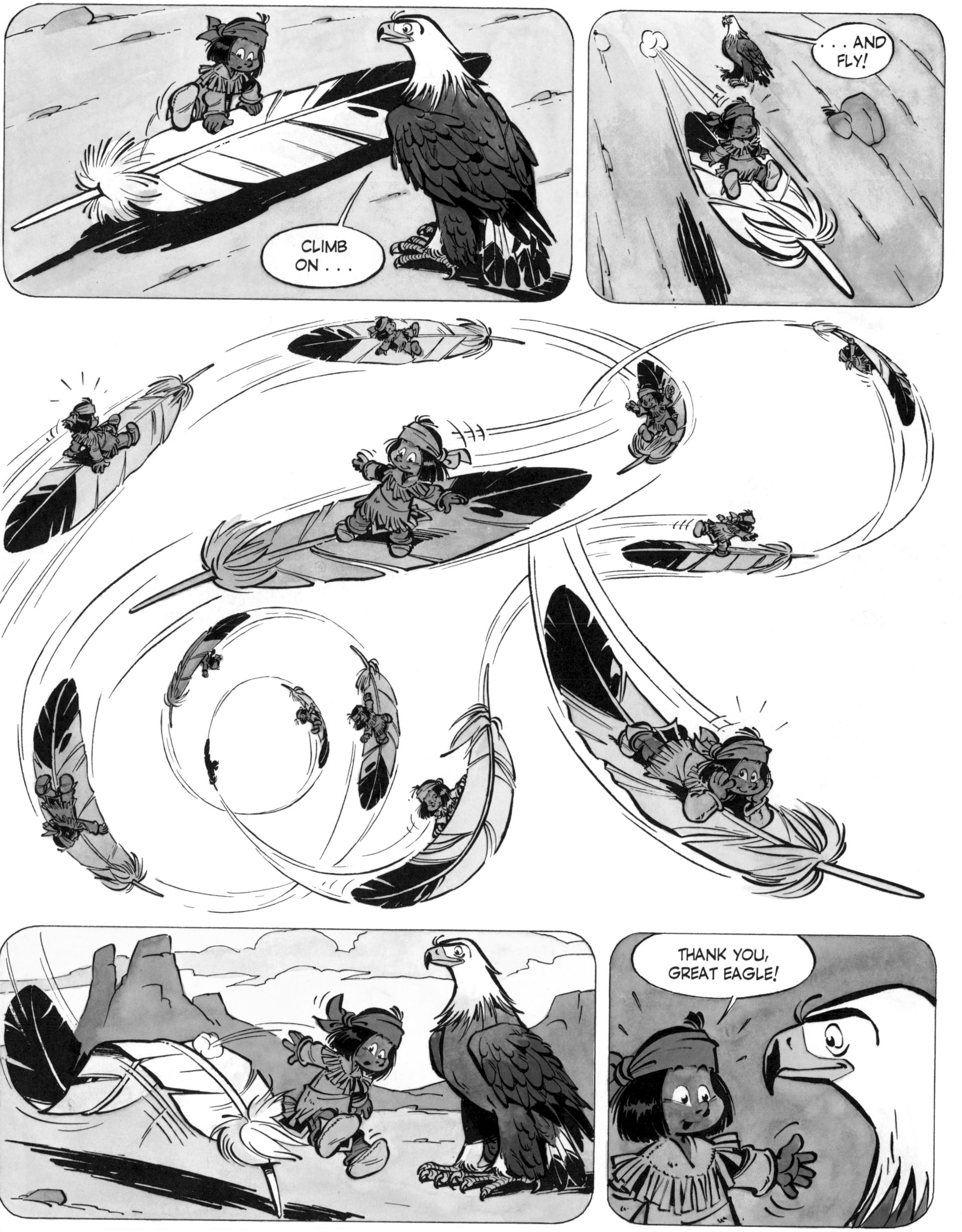
CLIMB ON . . .
. . . AND FLY!
THANK YOU, GREAT EAGLE!

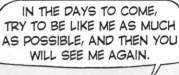

YOU'RE LUCKY, GREAT EAGLE, TO BE ABLE TO FLY AS YOU WANT!

I KNOW, YAKARI . . .

THIS IS THE LAST TIME THAT I WILL COME TO YOU IN YOUR DREAMS . . .

I WON'T SEE YOU ANYMORE?

IN THE DAYS TO COME, TRY TO BE LIKE ME AS MUCH AS POSSIBLE, AND THEN YOU WILL SEE ME AGAIN.

I MUST BE LIKE GREAT EAGLE.

MAYBE IF I CLOSE MY EYES . . .

IS THAT YOU ALREADY, GREAT EAGLE?

NO, IT'S YOUR MOTHER WHO IS WAITING FOR YOU TO FETCH WATER FROM THE RIVER.

6

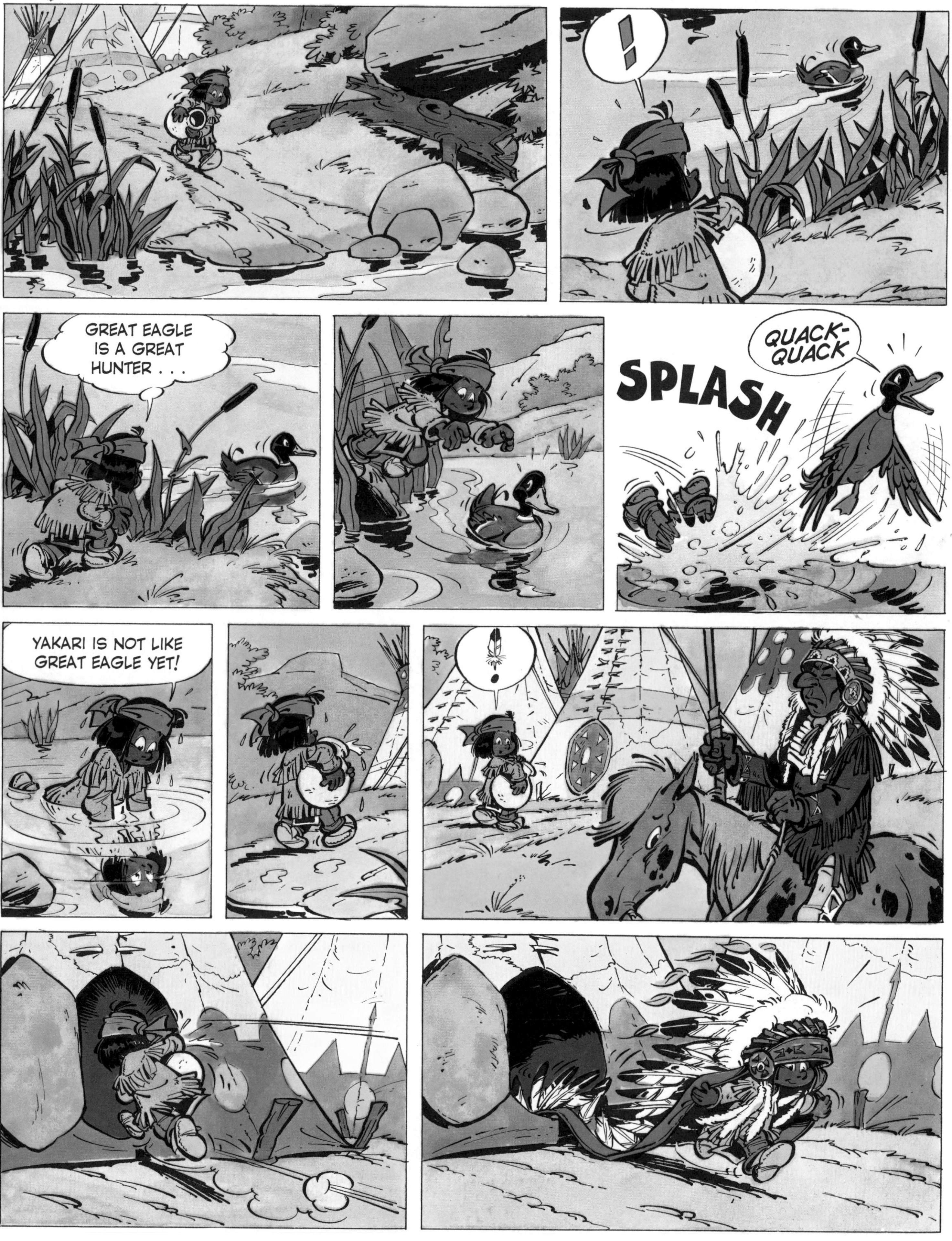
!
GREAT EAGLE IS A GREAT HUNTER . . .
SPLASH
QUACK-QUACK
YAKARI IS NOT LIKE GREAT EAGLE YET!
!

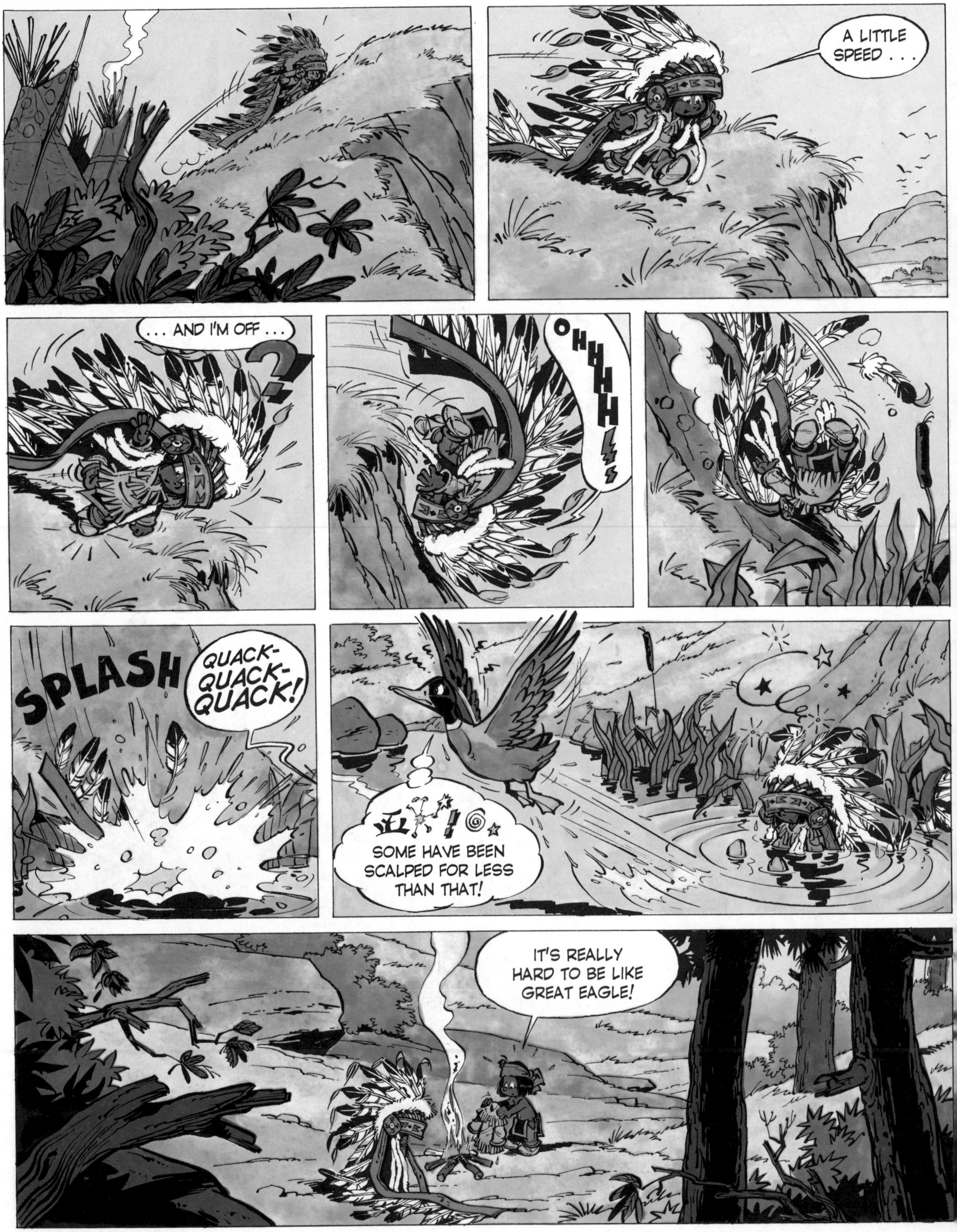

A LITTLE SPEED . . .
. . . AND I'M OFF . . .
?
OHHHHHH!
SPLASH
QUACK-QUACK-QUACK!
SOME HAVE BEEN SCALPED FOR LESS THAN THAT!
IT'S REALLY HARD TO BE LIKE GREAT EAGLE!

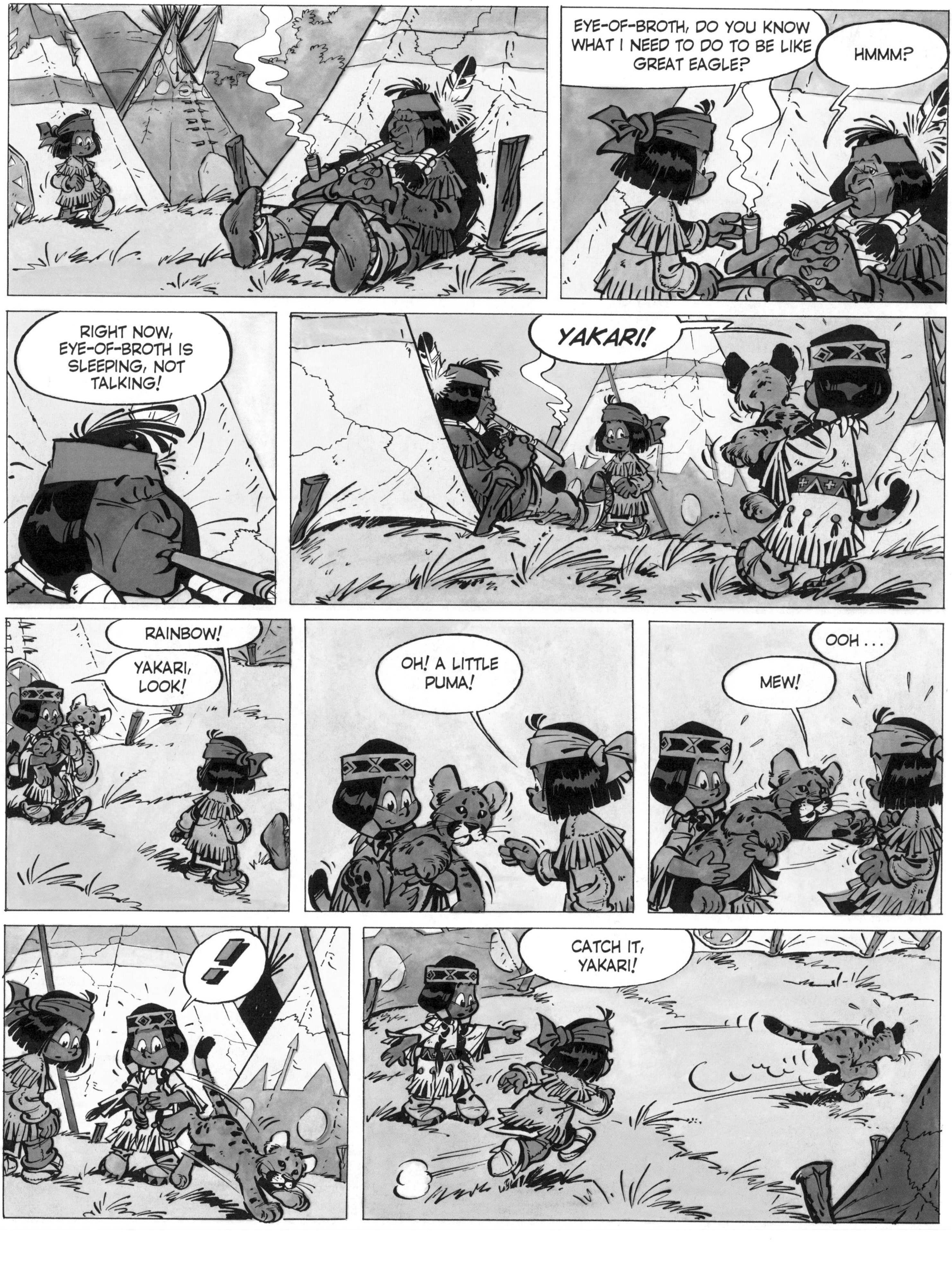
EYE-OF-BROTH, DO YOU KNOW WHAT I NEED TO DO TO BE LIKE GREAT EAGLE?
HMMM?
RIGHT NOW, EYE-OF-BROTH IS SLEEPING, NOT TALKING!
YAKARI!
RAINBOW!
YAKARI, LOOK!
OH! A LITTLE PUMA!
OOH . . .
MEW!
!
CATCH IT, YAKARI!

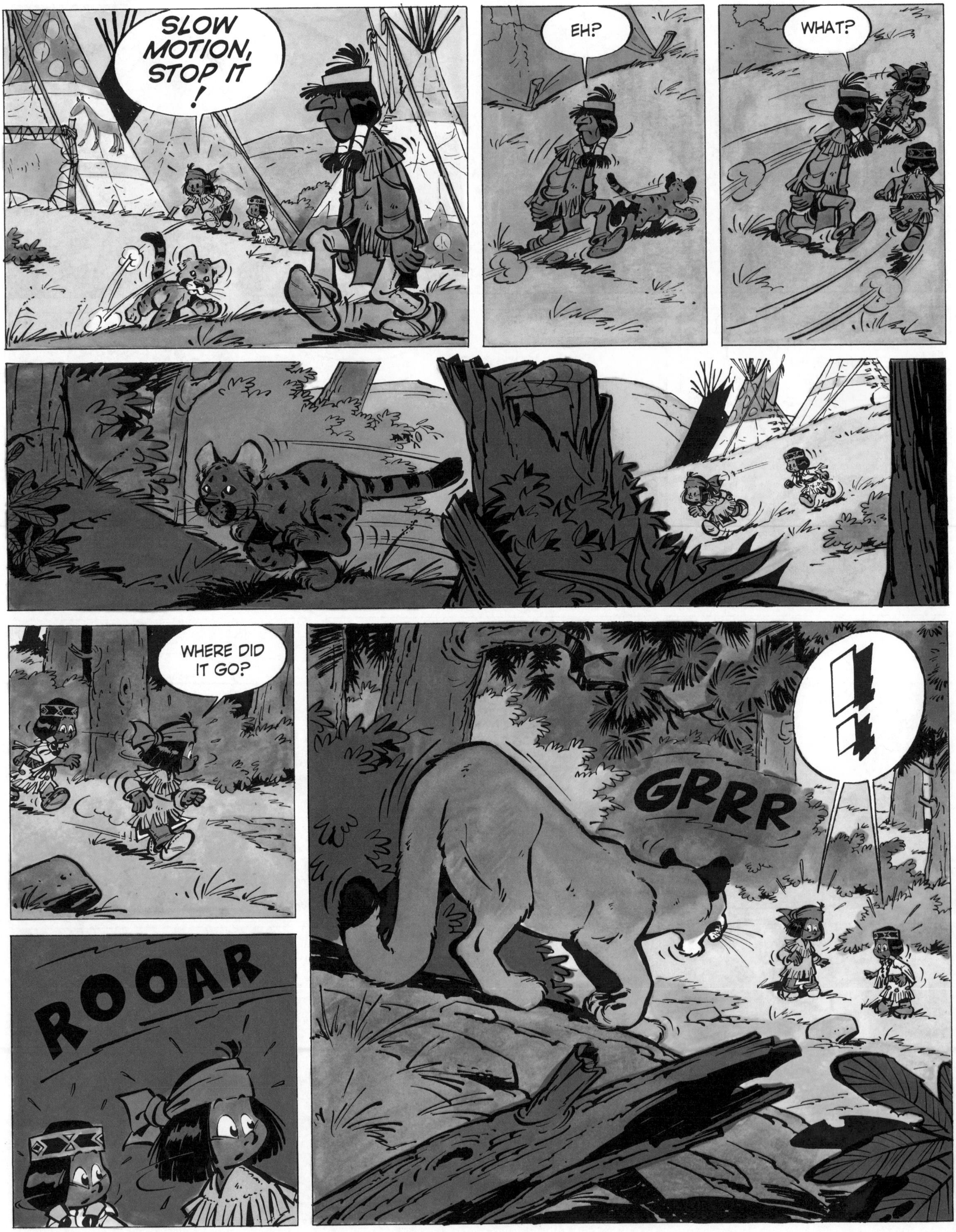
SLOW MOTION, STOP IT !
EH?
WHAT?
WHERE DID IT GO?
GRRR
!!
ROOAR

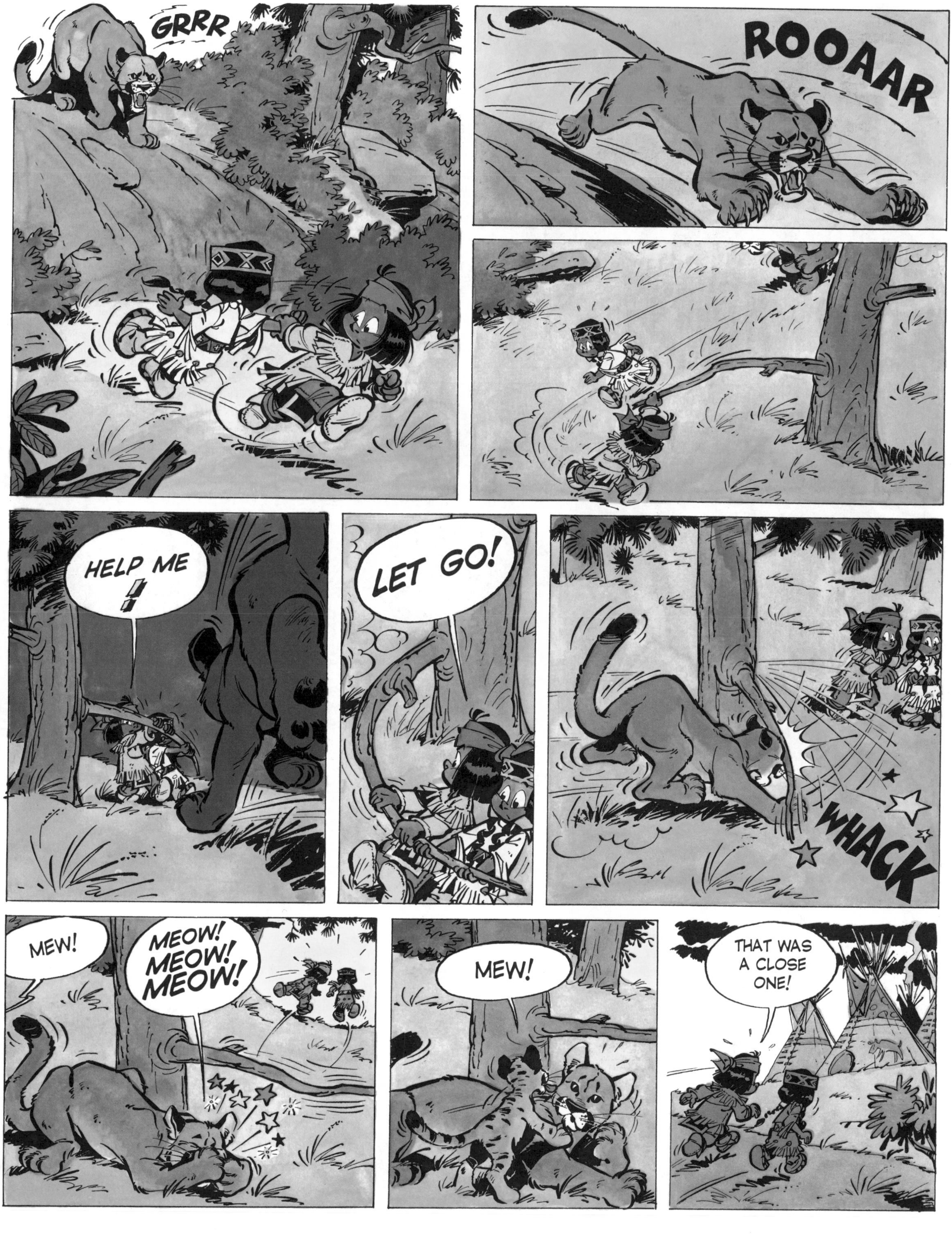
GRRR
ROOAAR
HELP ME!
LET GO!
WHACK
MEW!
MEOW! MEOW! MEOW!
MEW!
THAT WAS A CLOSE ONE!

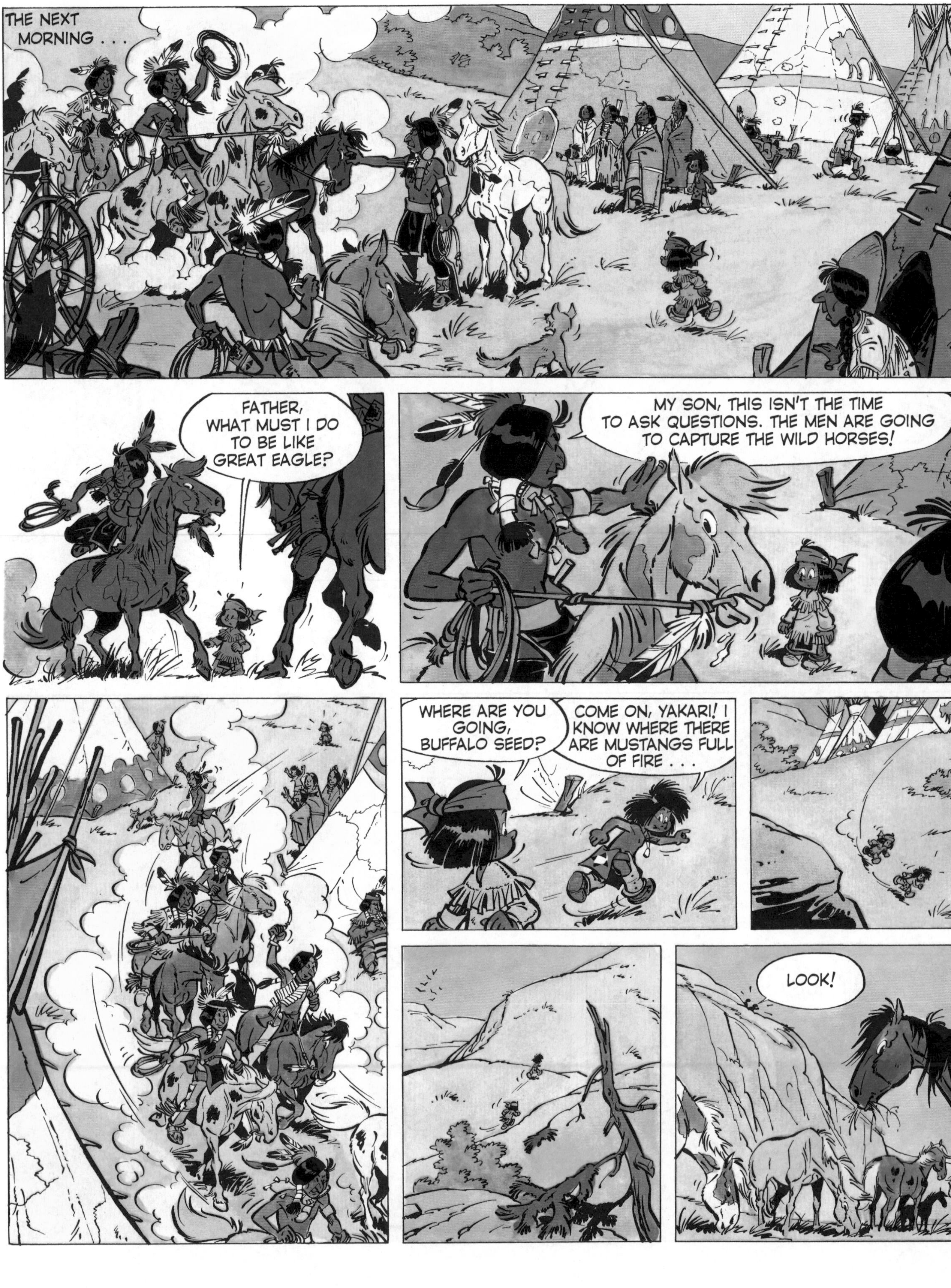

THE NEXT MORNING . . .
FATHER, WHAT MUST I DO TO BE LIKE GREAT EAGLE?
MY SON, THIS ISN'T THE TIME TO ASK QUESTIONS. THE MEN ARE GOING TO CAPTURE THE WILD HORSES!
WHERE ARE YOU GOING, BUFFALO SEED?
COME ON, YAKARI! I KNOW WHERE THERE ARE MUSTANGS FULL OF FIRE . . .
LOOK!

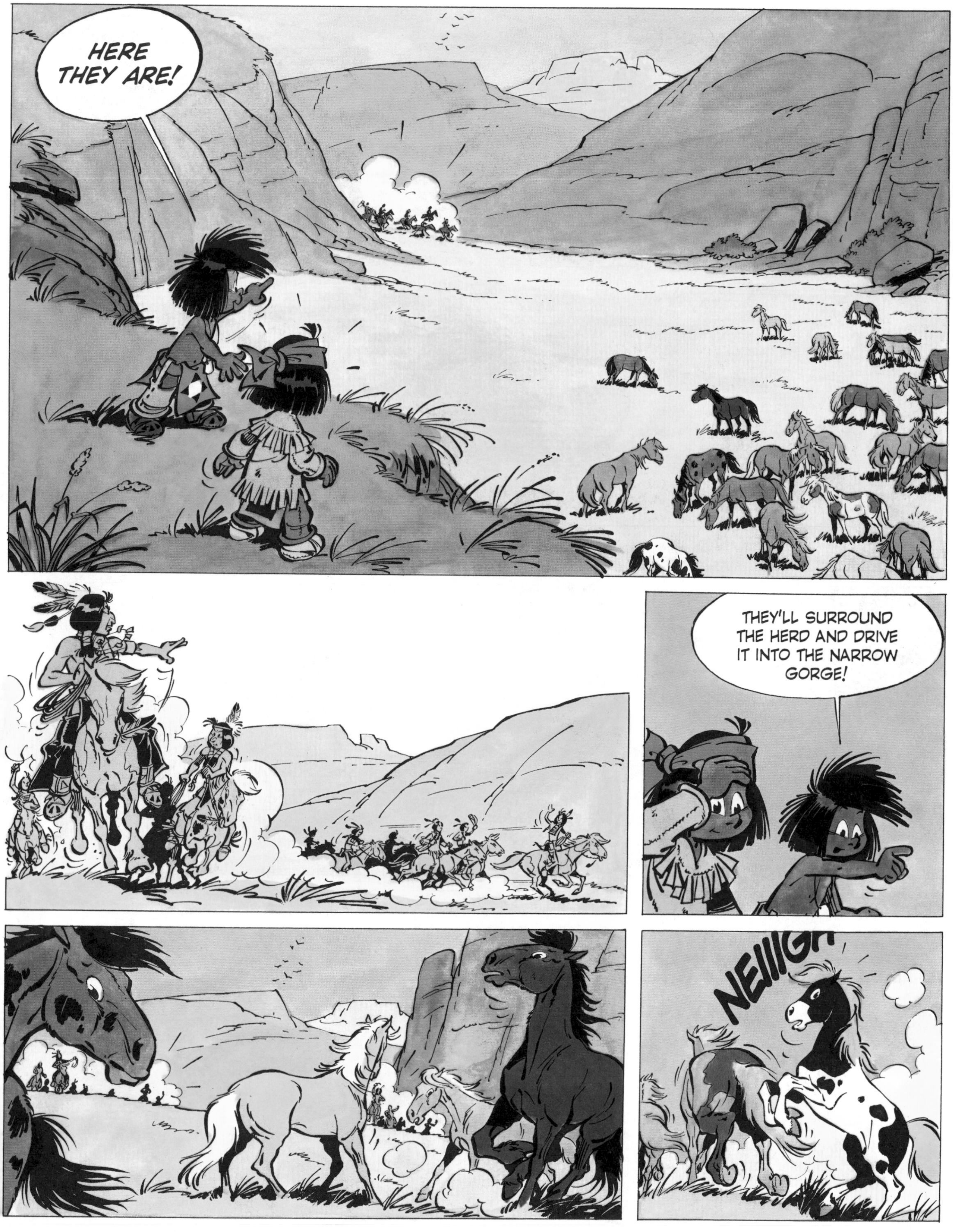
HERE THEY ARE!
THEY'LL SURROUND THE HERD AND DRIVE IT INTO THE NARROW GORGE!
NEIIIGH

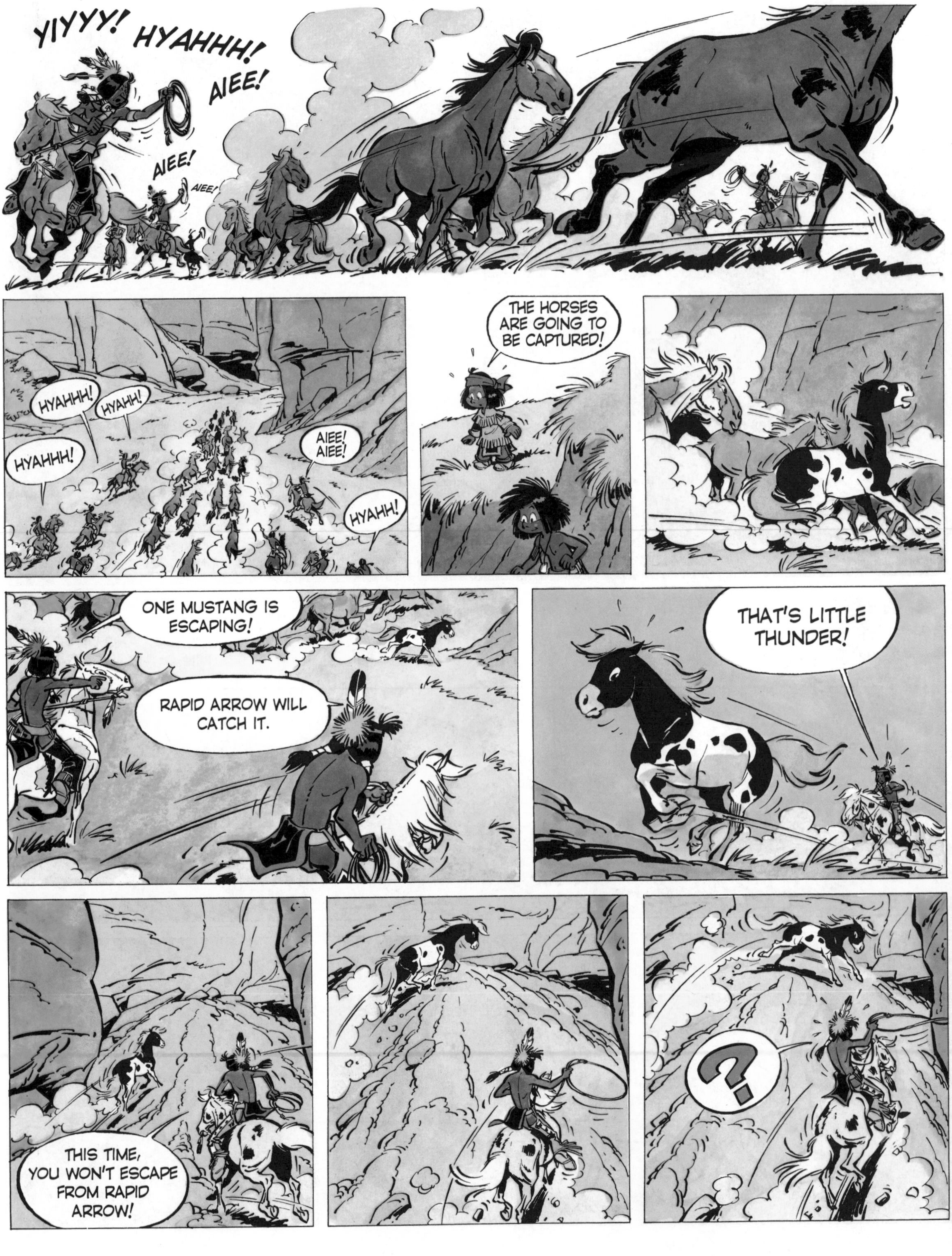
YIYYY! HYAHHH!
AIEE!
AIEE!
AIEE!
HYAHHH!
HYAHH!
HYAHHH!
AIEE! AIEE!
HYAHH!
THE HORSES ARE GOING TO BE CAPTURED!
ONE MUSTANG IS ESCAPING!
RAPID ARROW WILL CATCH IT.
THAT'S LITTLE THUNDER!
THIS TIME, YOU WON'T ESCAPE FROM RAPID ARROW!
?

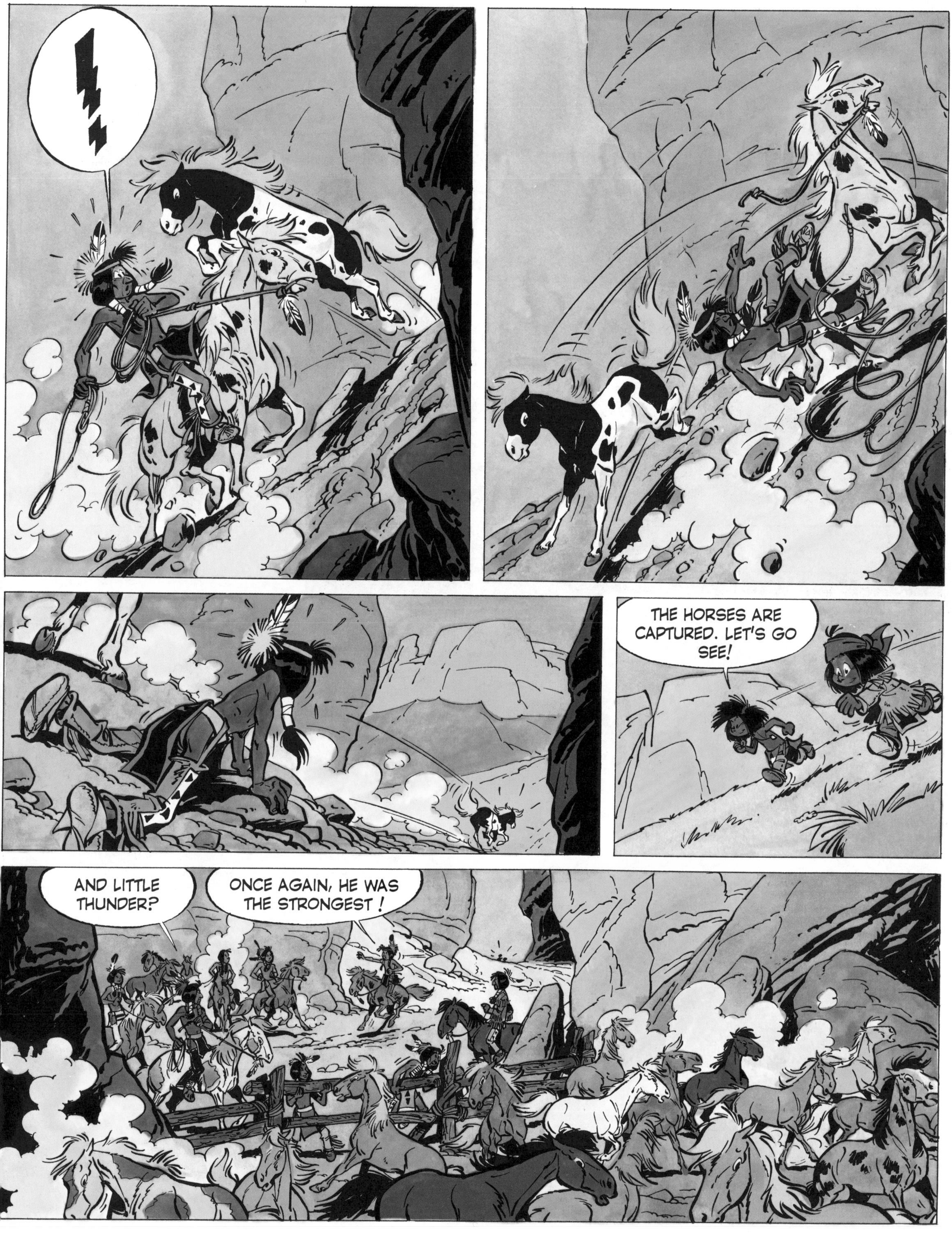
!
THE HORSES ARE CAPTURED. LET'S GO SEE!
AND LITTLE THUNDER?
ONCE AGAIN, HE WAS THE STRONGEST !

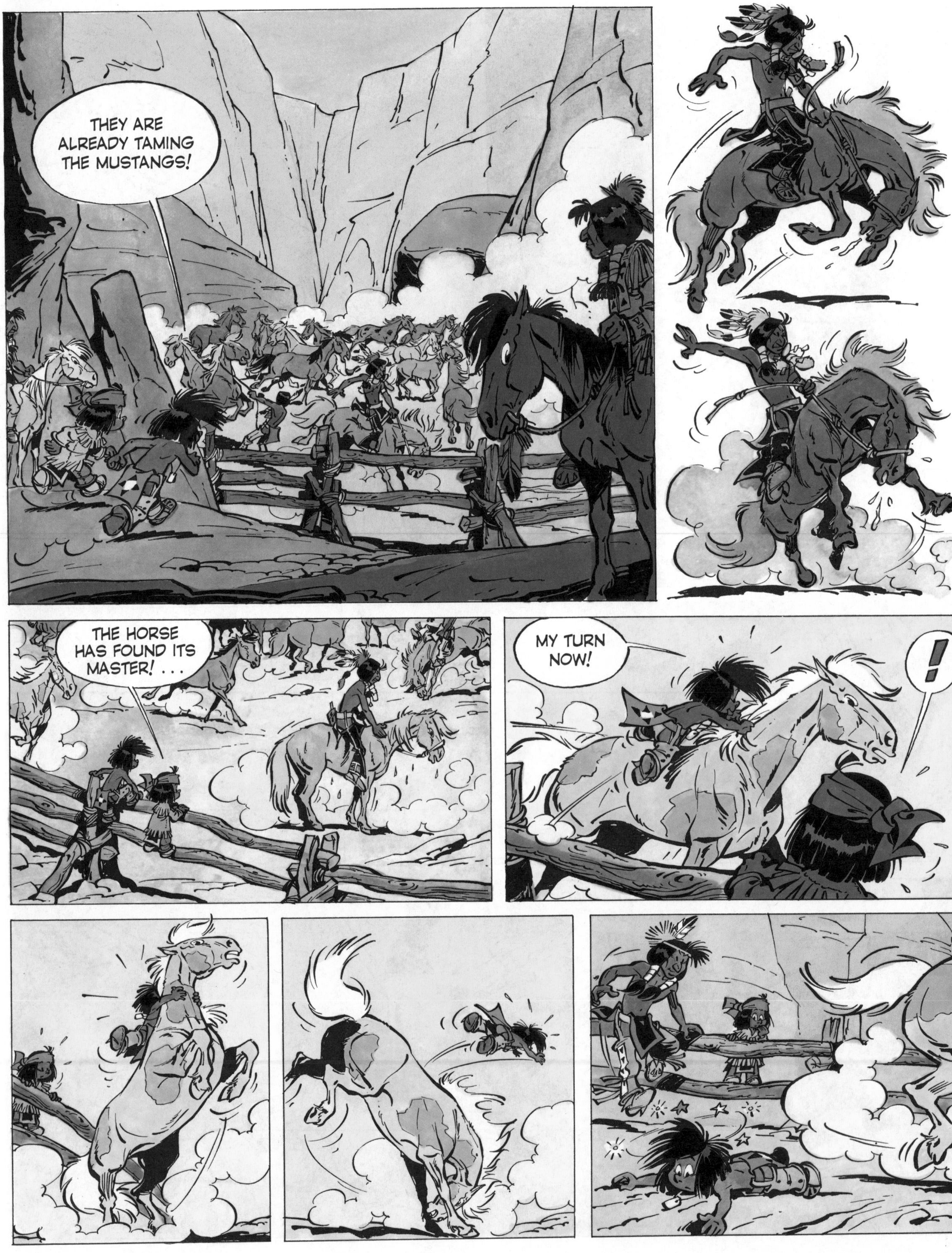
THEY ARE ALREADY TAMING THE MUSTANGS!
THE HORSE HAS FOUND ITS MASTER! . . .
MY TURN NOW!
!

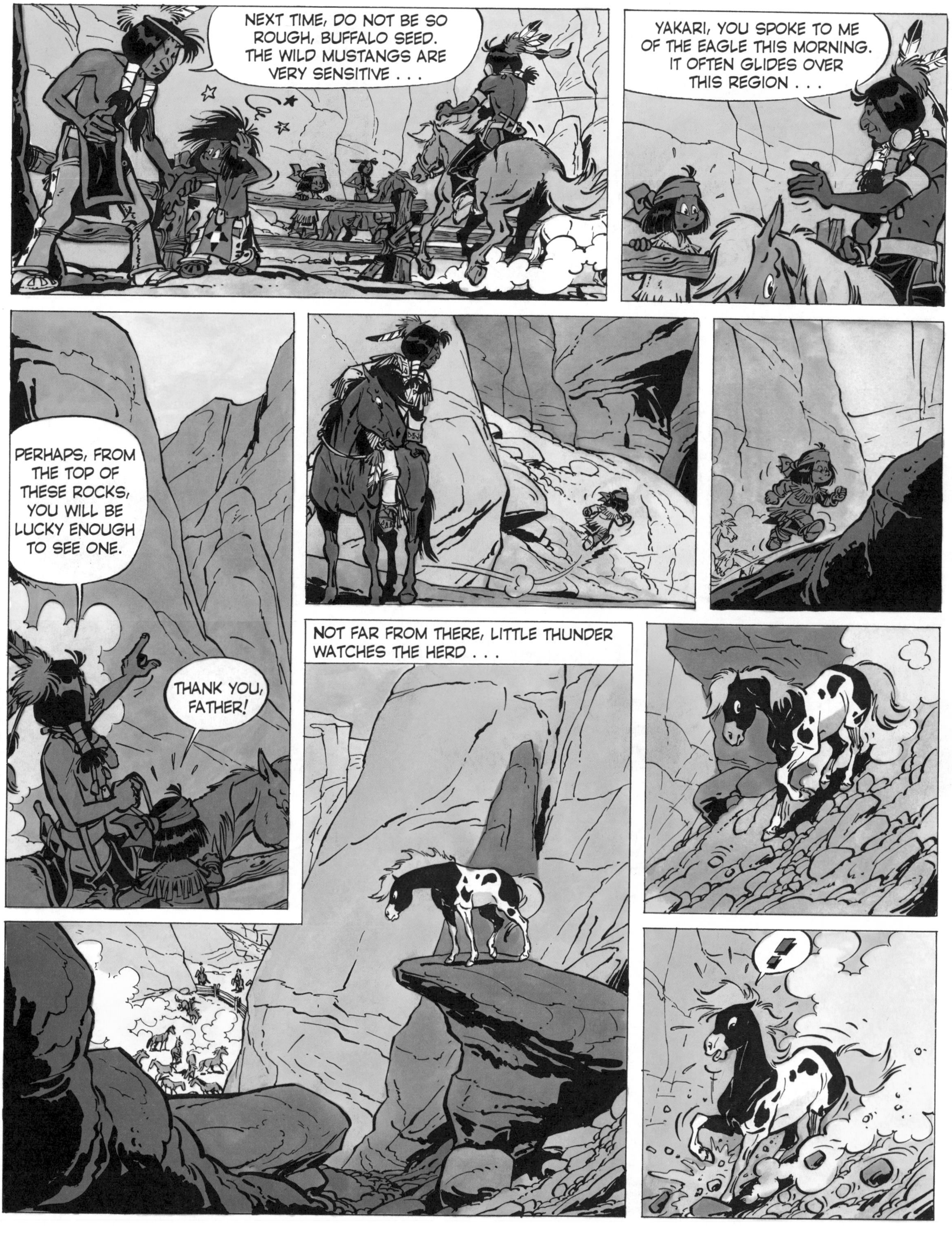
NEXT TIME, DO NOT BE SO ROUGH, BUFFALO SEED. THE WILD MUSTANGS ARE VERY SENSITIVE . . .
YAKARI, YOU SPOKE TO ME OF THE EAGLE THIS MORNING. IT OFTEN GLIDES OVER THIS REGION . . .
PERHAPS, FROM THE TOP OF THESE ROCKS, YOU WILL BE LUCKY ENOUGH TO SEE ONE.
THANK YOU, FATHER!
NOT FAR FROM THERE, LITTLE THUNDER WATCHES THE HERD . . .
!

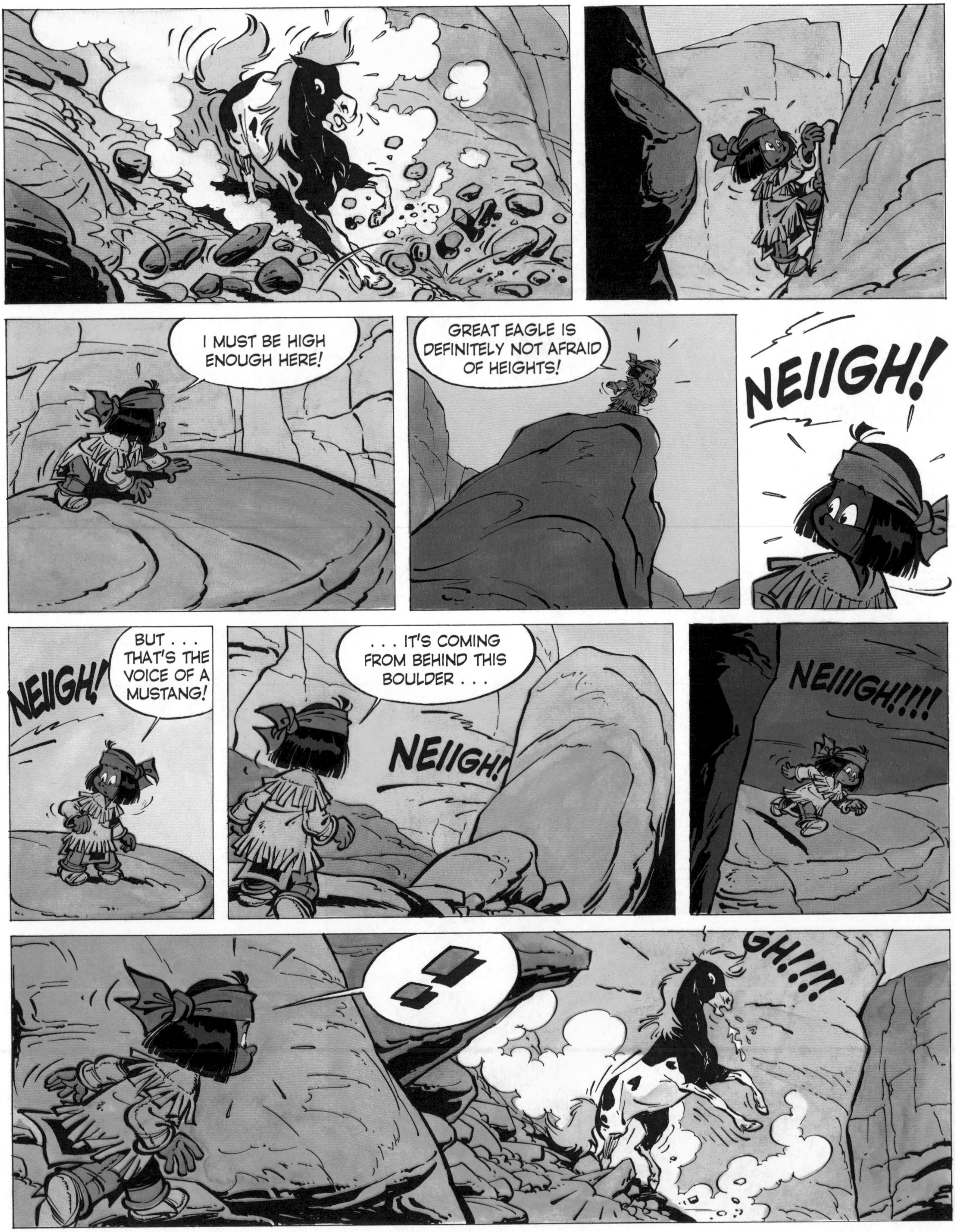
I MUST BE HIGH ENOUGH HERE!
GREAT EAGLE IS DEFINITELY NOT AFRAID OF HEIGHTS!
NEIIGH!
NEIIGH!
BUT . . . THAT'S THE VOICE OF A MUSTANG!
. . . IT'S COMING FROM BEHIND THIS BOULDER . . .
NEIIGH!
NEIIIGH!!!!!
GH!!!!!

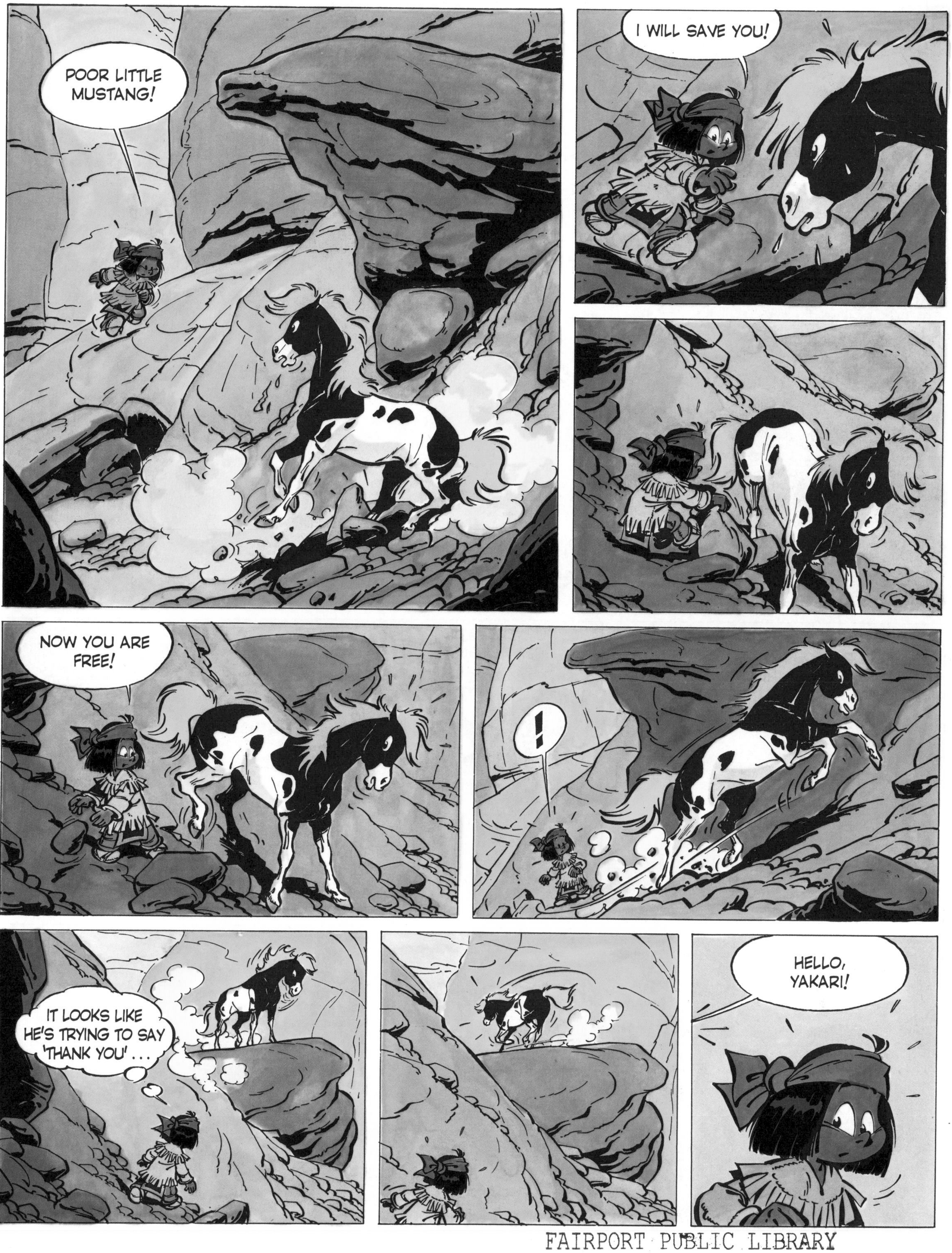
POOR LITTLE MUSTANG!
I WILL SAVE YOU!
NOW YOU ARE FREE!
!
IT LOOKS LIKE HE'S TRYING TO SAY 'THANK YOU' . . .
HELLO, YAKARI!

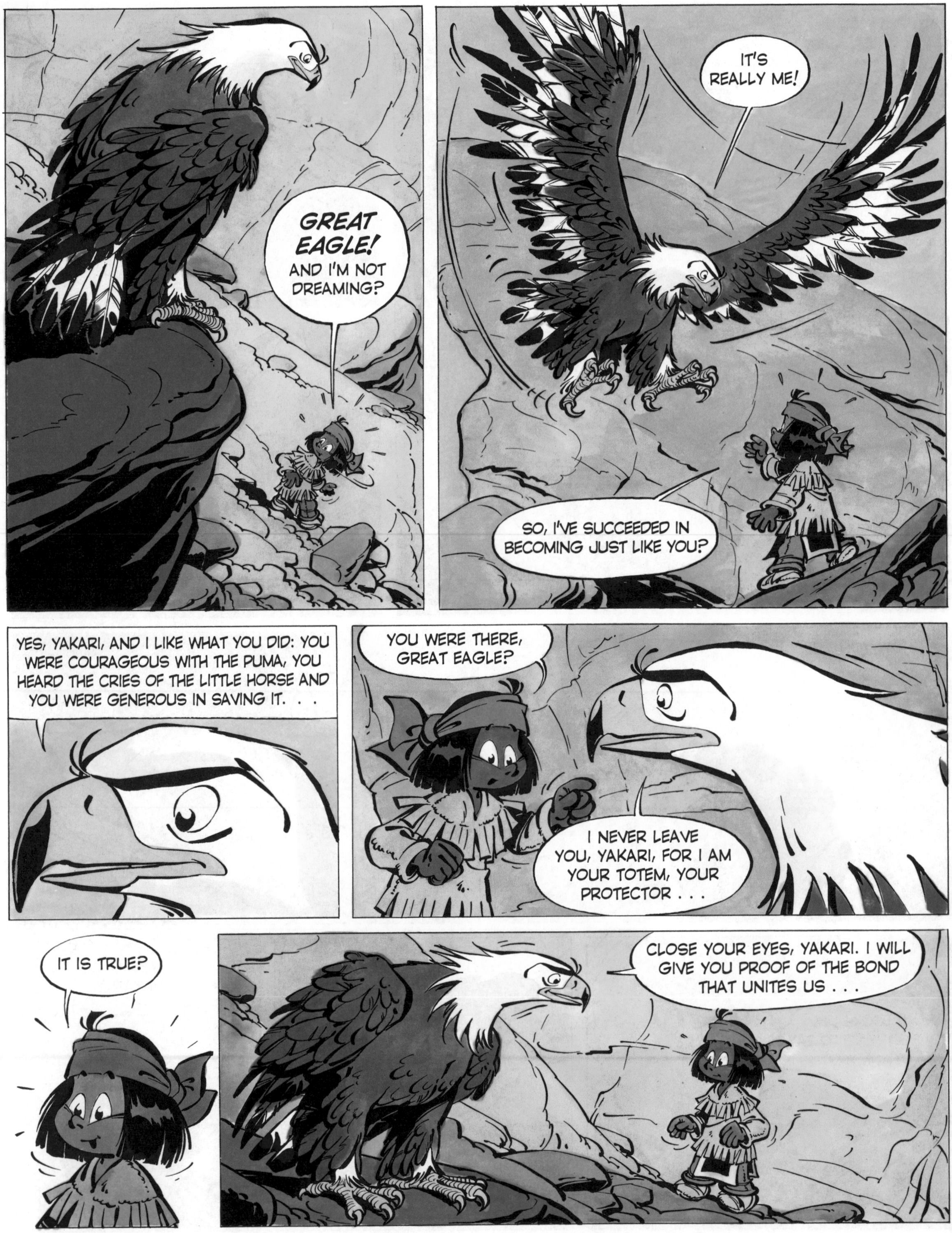
GREAT EAGLE! AND I'M NOT DREAMING?
IT'S REALLY ME!
SO, I'VE SUCCEEDED IN BECOMING JUST LIKE YOU?
YES, YAKARI, AND I LIKE WHAT YOU DID: YOU WERE COURAGEOUS WITH THE PUMA, YOU HEARD THE CRIES OF THE LITTLE HORSE AND YOU WERE GENEROUS IN SAVING IT. . .
YOU WERE THERE, GREAT EAGLE?
I NEVER LEAVE YOU, YAKARI, FOR I AM YOUR TOTEM, YOUR PROTECTOR . . .
IT IS TRUE?
CLOSE YOUR EYES, YAKARI. I WILL GIVE YOU PROOF OF THE BOND THAT UNITES US . . .

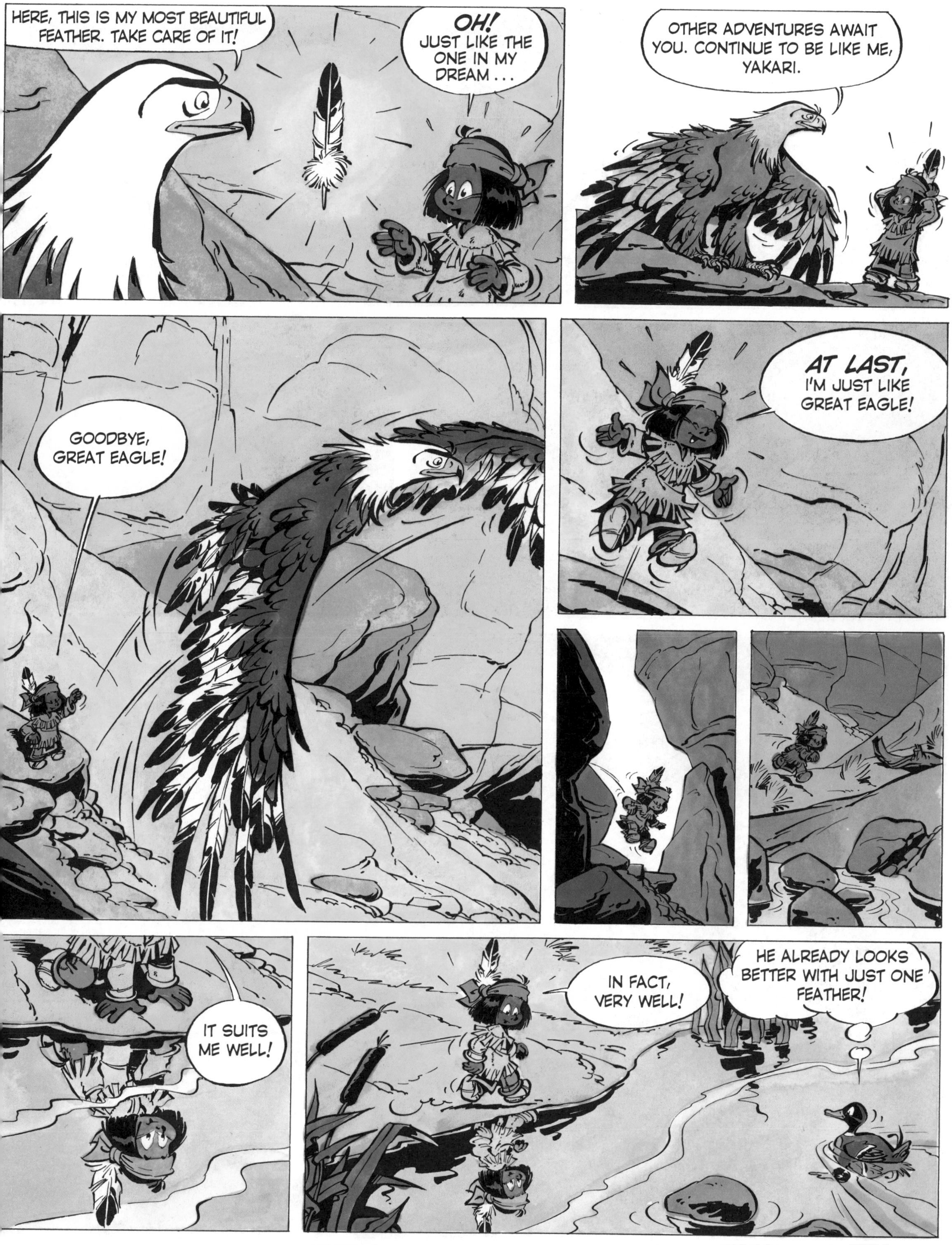
HERE, THIS IS MY MOST BEAUTIFUL FEATHER. TAKE CARE OF IT!
OH! JUST LIKE THE ONE IN MY DREAM . . .
OTHER ADVENTURES AWAIT YOU. CONTINUE TO BE LIKE ME, YAKARI.
GOODBYE, GREAT EAGLE!
AT LAST, I'M JUST LIKE GREAT EAGLE!
IT SUITS ME WELL!
IN FACT, VERY WELL!
HE ALREADY LOOKS BETTER WITH JUST ONE FEATHER!

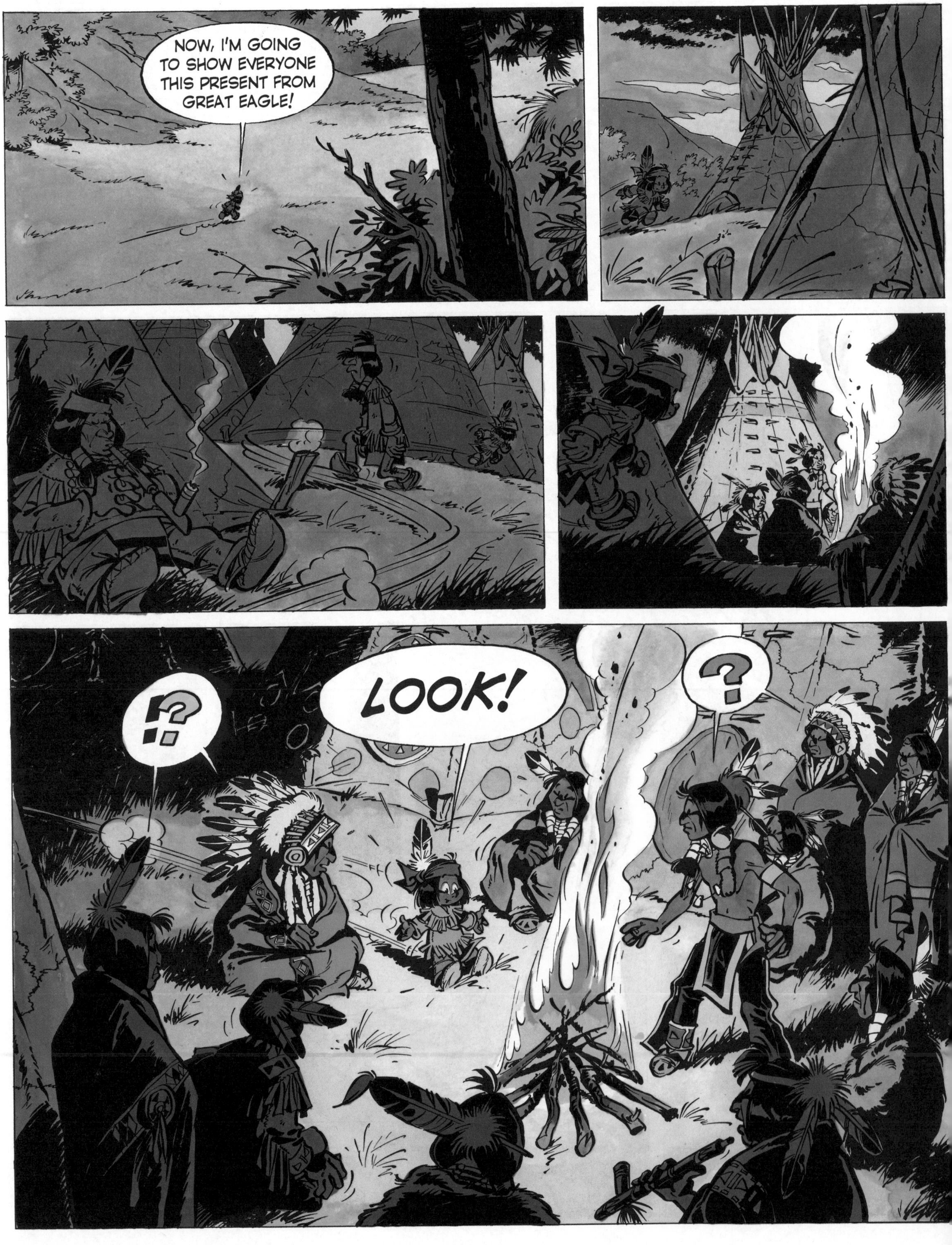
NOW, I'M GOING TO SHOW EVERYONE THIS PRESENT FROM GREAT EAGLE!
!?
LOOK!
?

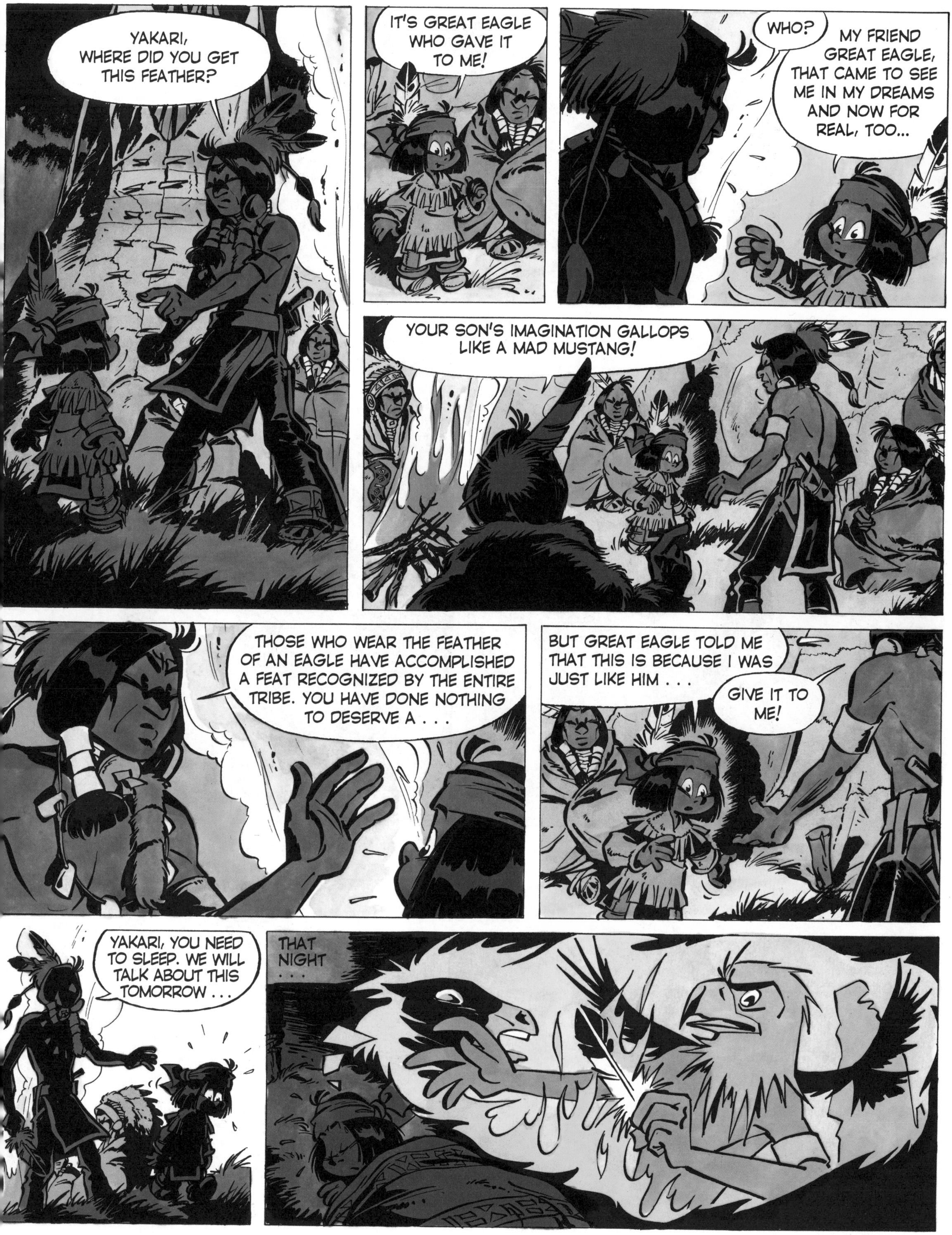
YAKARI, WHERE DID YOU GET THIS FEATHER?
IT'S GREAT EAGLE WHO GAVE IT TO ME!
WHO?
MY FRIEND GREAT EAGLE, THAT CAME TO SEE ME IN MY DREAMS AND NOW FOR REAL, TOO...
YOUR SON'S IMAGINATION GALLOPS LIKE A MAD MUSTANG!
THOSE WHO WEAR THE FEATHER OF AN EAGLE HAVE ACCOMPLISHED A FEAT RECOGNIZED BY THE ENTIRE TRIBE. YOU HAVE DONE NOTHING TO DESERVE A . . .
BUT GREAT EAGLE TOLD ME THAT THIS IS BECAUSE I WAS JUST LIKE HIM . . .
GIVE IT TO ME!
YAKARI, YOU NEED TO SLEEP. WE WILL TALK ABOUT THIS TOMORROW . . .
THAT NIGHT . . .

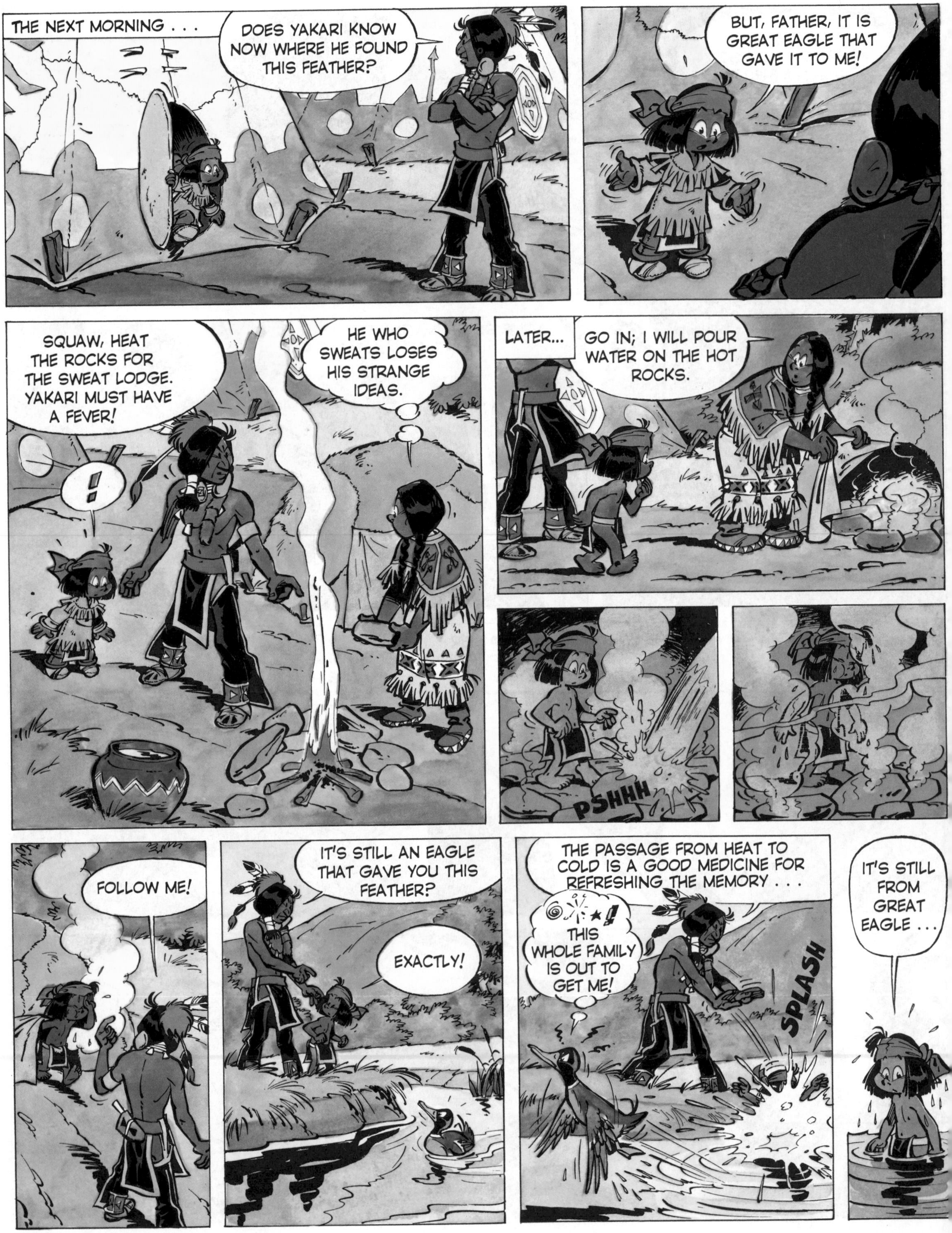
THE NEXT MORNING . . .
DOES YAKARI KNOW NOW WHERE HE FOUND THIS FEATHER?
BUT, FATHER, IT IS GREAT EAGLE THAT GAVE IT TO ME!
SQUAW, HEAT THE ROCKS FOR THE SWEAT LODGE. YAKARI MUST HAVE A FEVER!
HE WHO SWEATS LOSES HIS STRANGE IDEAS.
!
LATER...
GO IN; I WILL POUR WATER ON THE HOT ROCKS.
PSHHH
FOLLOW ME!
IT'S STILL AN EAGLE THAT GAVE YOU THIS FEATHER?
EXACTLY!
THE PASSAGE FROM HEAT TO COLD IS A GOOD MEDICINE FOR REFRESHING THE MEMORY . . .
THIS WHOLE FAMILY IS OUT TO GET ME!
SPLASH
IT'S STILL FROM GREAT EAGLE . . .

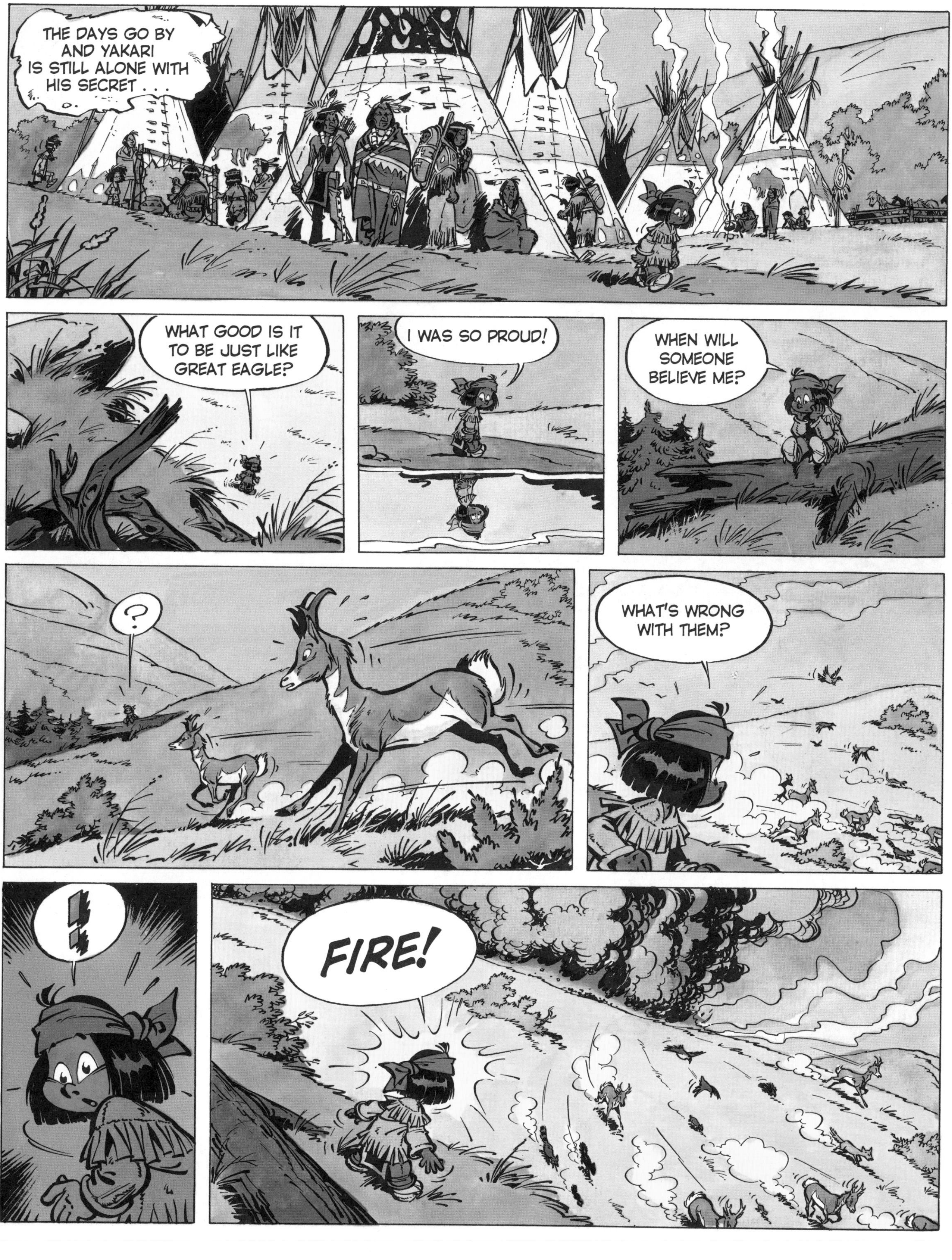
THE DAYS GO BY AND YAKARI IS STILL ALONE WITH HIS SECRET . . .
WHAT GOOD IS IT TO BE JUST LIKE GREAT EAGLE?
I WAS SO PROUD!
WHEN WILL SOMEONE BELIEVE ME?
?
WHAT'S WRONG WITH THEM?
!
FIRE!

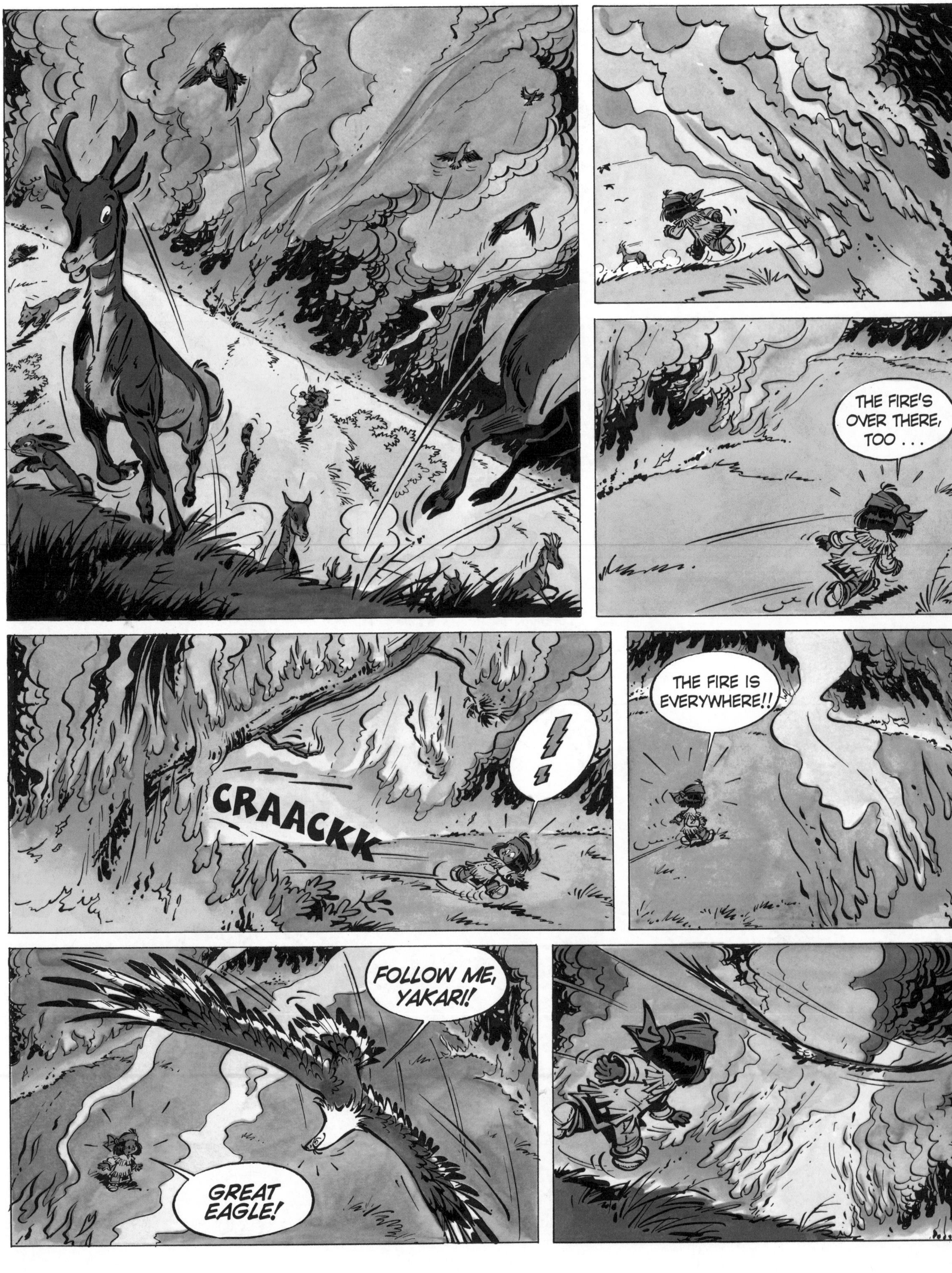
THE FIRE'S OVER THERE, TOO . . .
CRAACKK
!
THE FIRE IS EVERYWHERE!!
FOLLOW ME, YAKARI!
GREAT EAGLE!

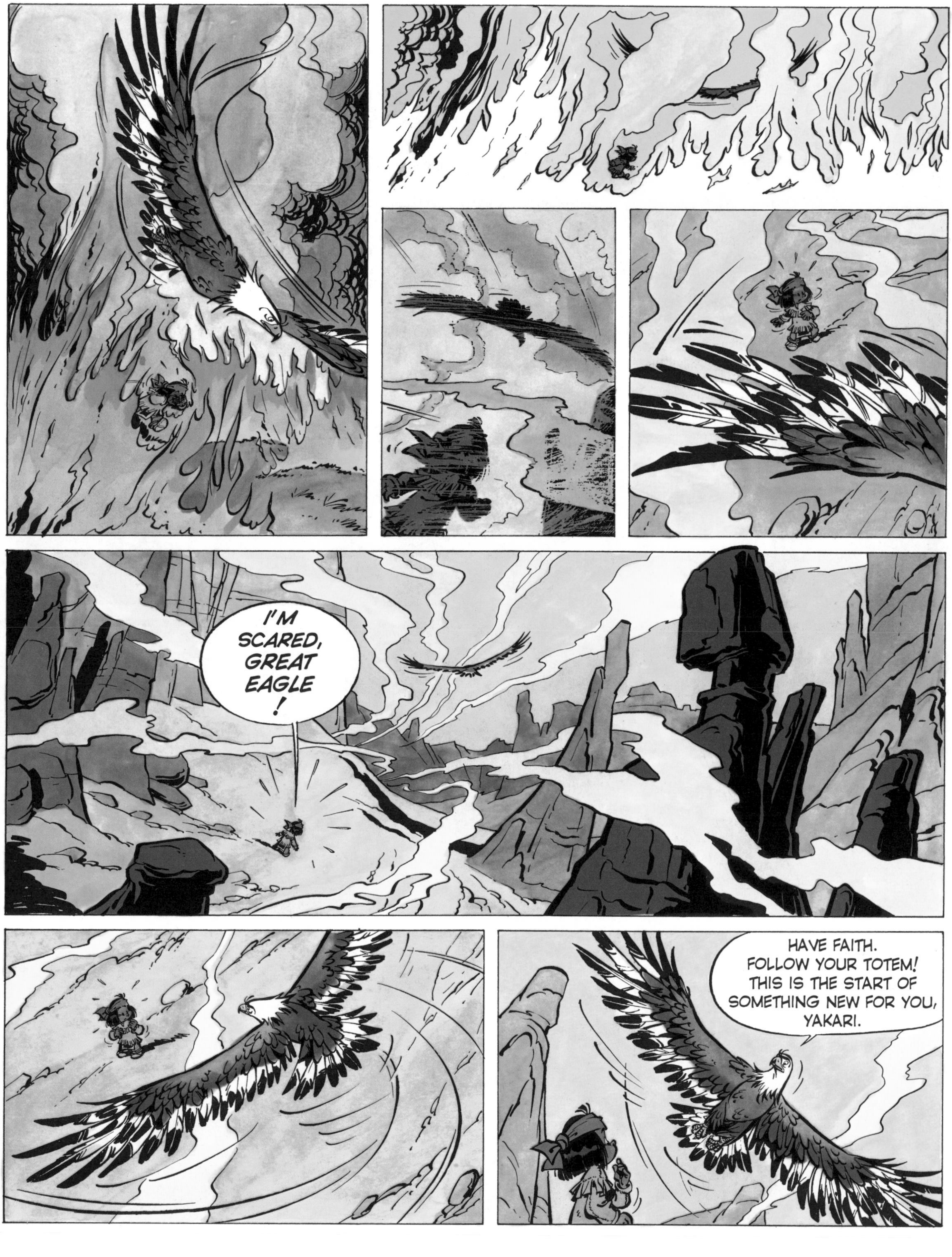
I'M SCARED, GREAT EAGLE !
HAVE FAITH. FOLLOW YOUR TOTEM! THIS IS THE START OF SOMETHING NEW FOR YOU, YAKARI.

NIGHT IS COMING. WE WILL STOP.

GREAT EAGLE, COULD YOU TELL ME WHY THE PEOPLE OF MY TRIBE DID NOT BELIEVE ME?

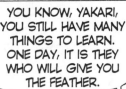

YOU KNOW, YAKARI, YOU STILL HAVE MANY THINGS TO LEARN. ONE DAY, IT IS THEY WHO WILL GIVE YOU THE FEATHER.

HOW? THEM? WHY?

PATIENCE, YAKARI . . . AND NOW, SLEEP!

IN THE MEANTIME . . .

NO TRACKS FROM YOUR SON . . .

LET US RETURN TO CAMP. PERHAPS WE WILL FIND YAKARI THERE . . .

THE NEXT MORNING . . .

!

CRUNCH

MMM

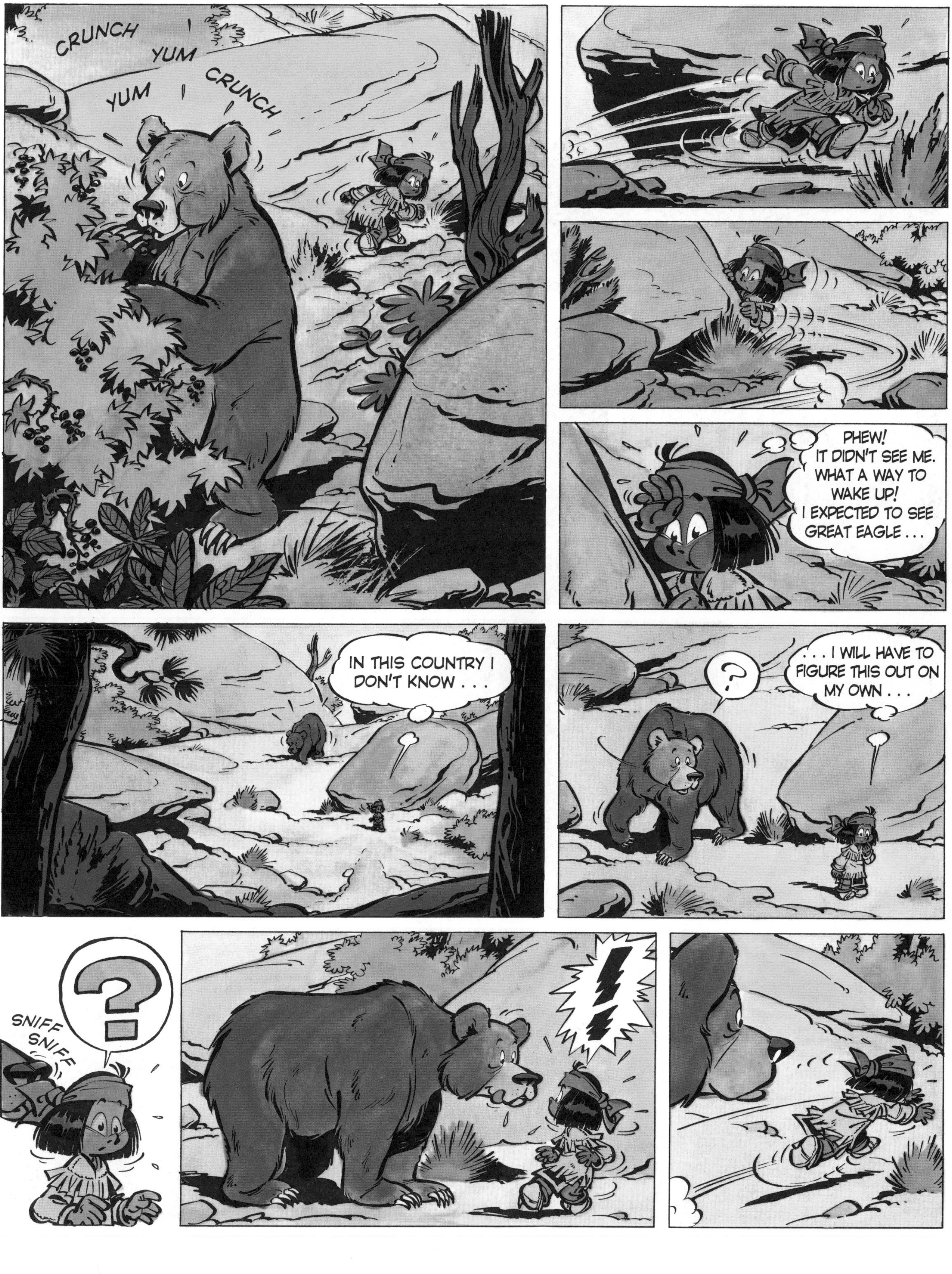
CRUNCH
YUM
YUM
CRUNCH
PHEW! IT DIDN'T SEE ME. WHAT A WAY TO WAKE UP! I EXPECTED TO SEE GREAT EAGLE . . .
IN THIS COUNTRY I DON'T KNOW . . .
?
. . . I WILL HAVE TO FIGURE THIS OUT ON MY OWN . . .
SNIFF SNIFF
?

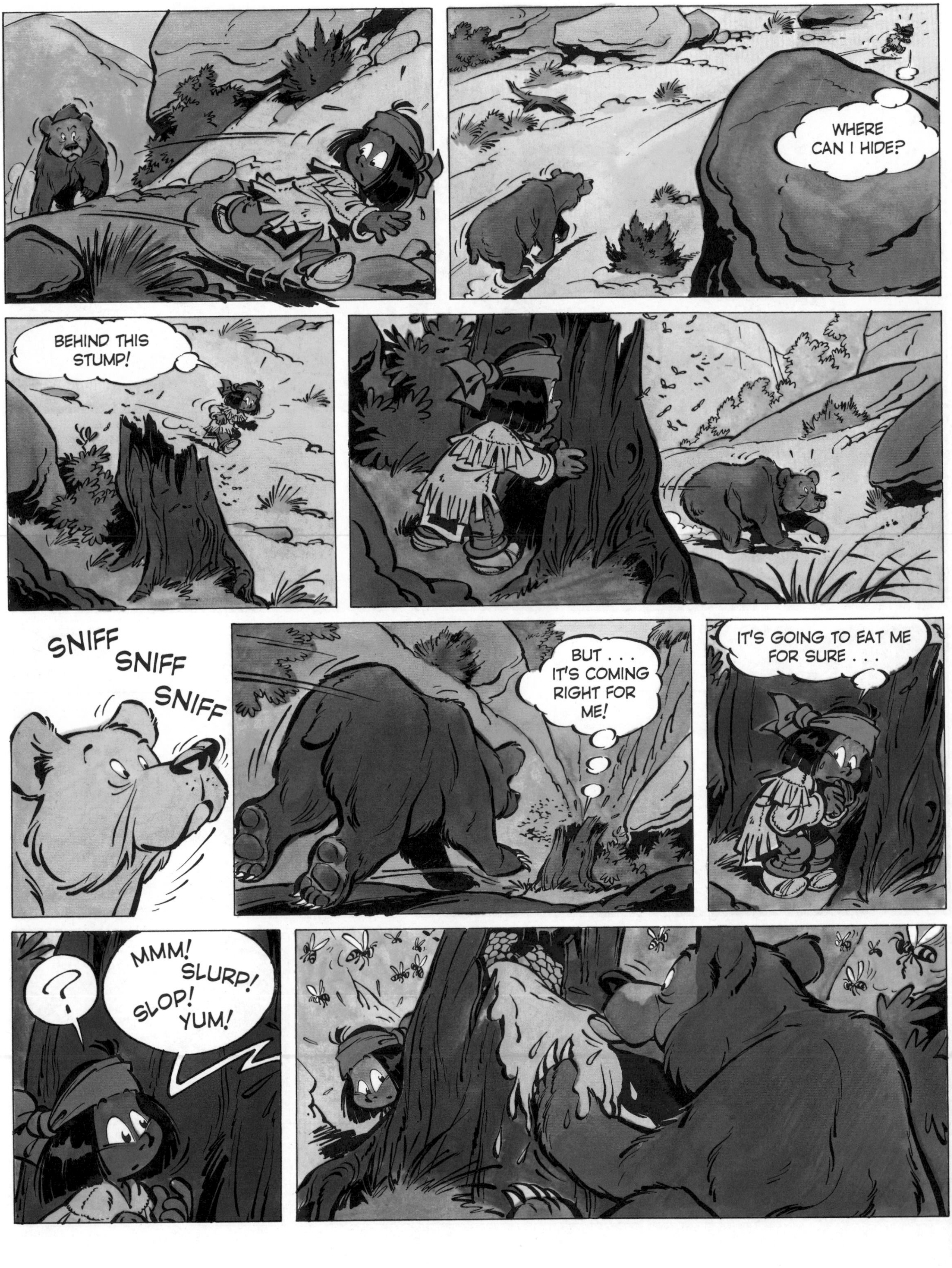
WHERE CAN I HIDE?
BEHIND THIS STUMP!
SNIFF SNIFF SNIFF
BUT . . . IT'S COMING RIGHT FOR ME!
IT'S GOING TO EAT ME FOR SURE . . .
?
MMM! SLURP! SLOP! YUM!

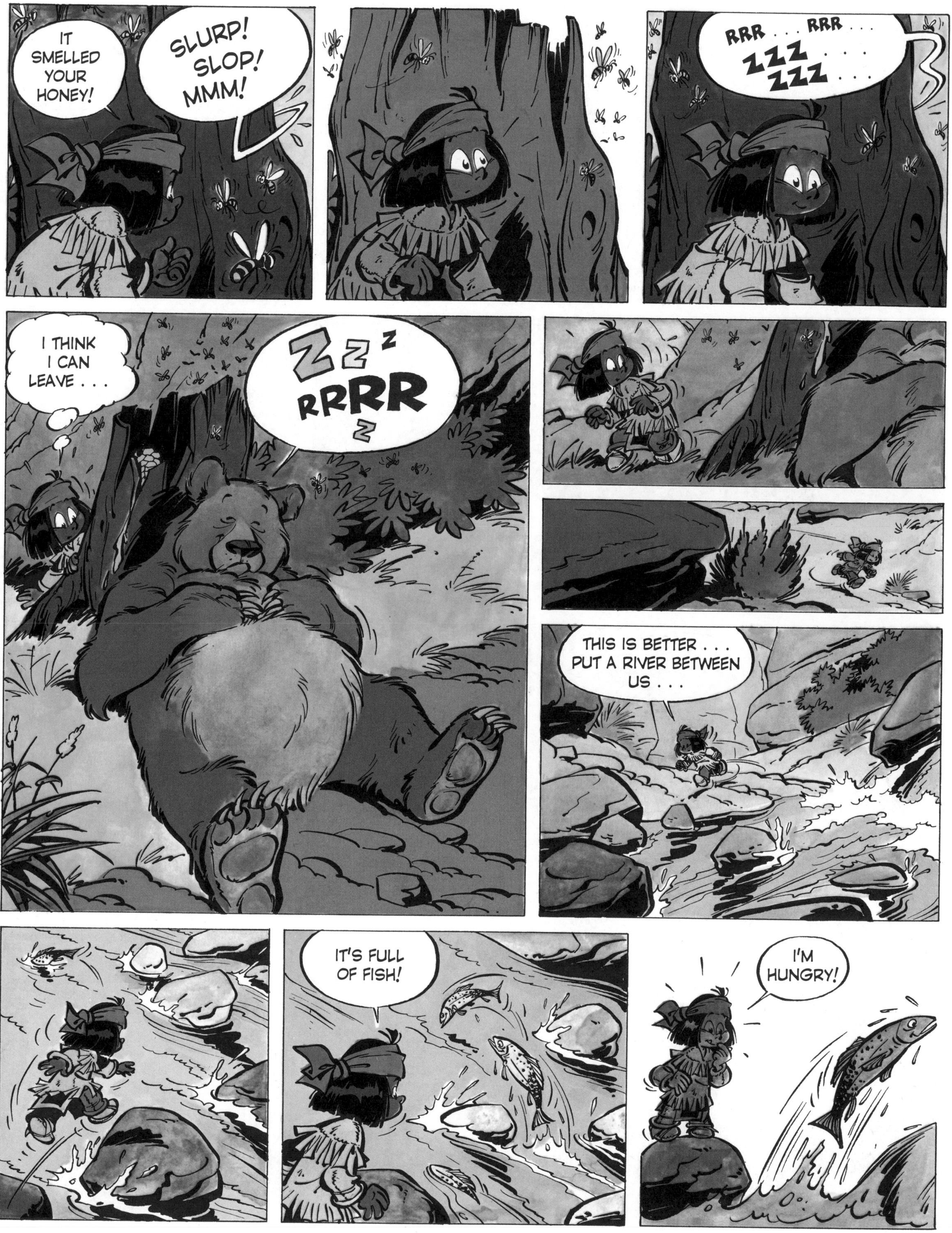
IT SMELLED YOUR HONEY!
SLURP! SLOP! MMM!
RRR . . . RRR . . . ZZZ . . . ZZZ . . .
I THINK I CAN LEAVE . . .
ZZZ RRRR Z
THIS IS BETTER . . . PUT A RIVER BETWEEN US . . .
IT'S FULL OF FISH!
I'M HUNGRY!

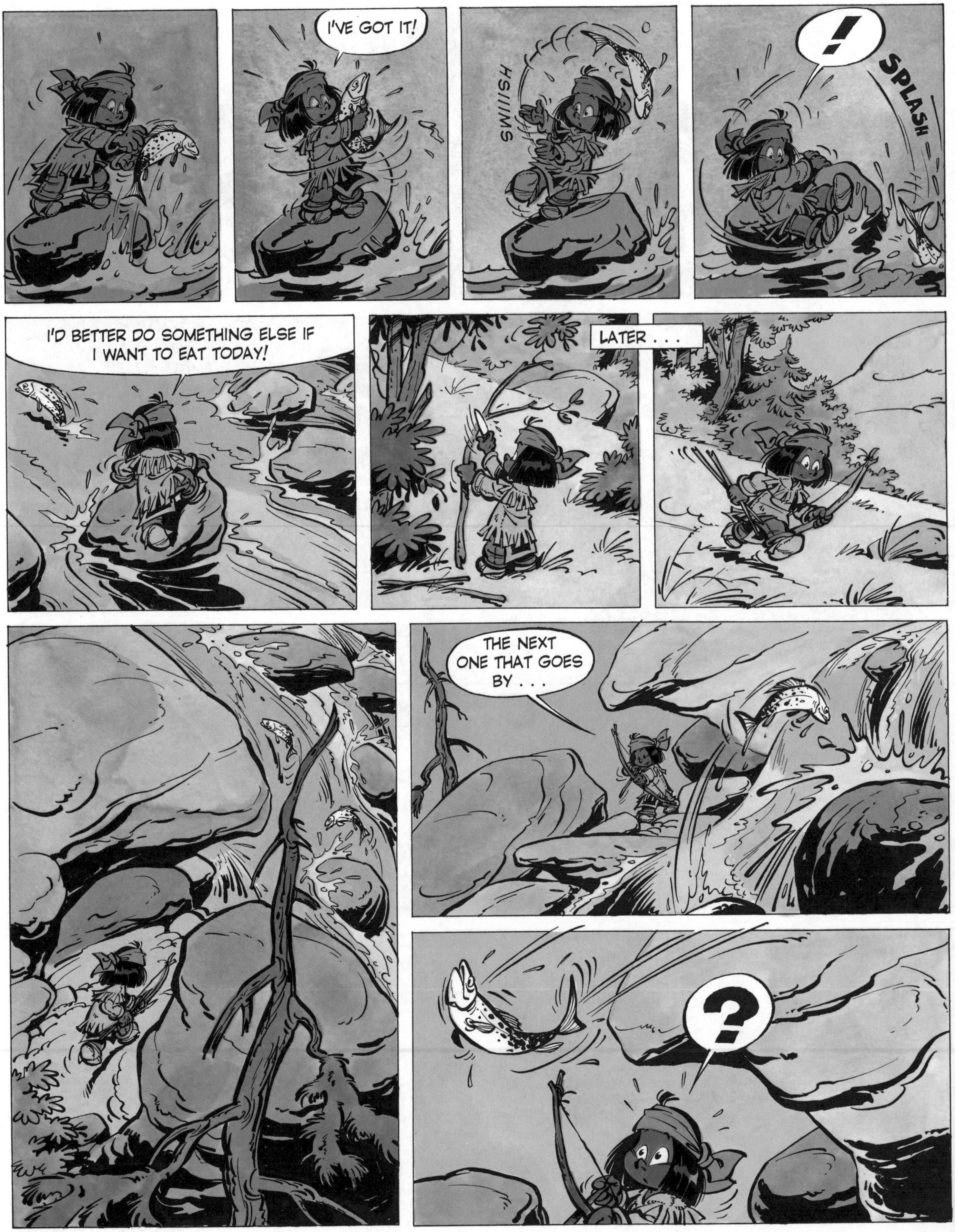
I'VE GOT IT!
SWIIISH
!
SPLASH
I'D BETTER DO SOMETHING ELSE IF I WANT TO EAT TODAY!
LATER . . .
THE NEXT ONE THAT GOES BY . . .
?

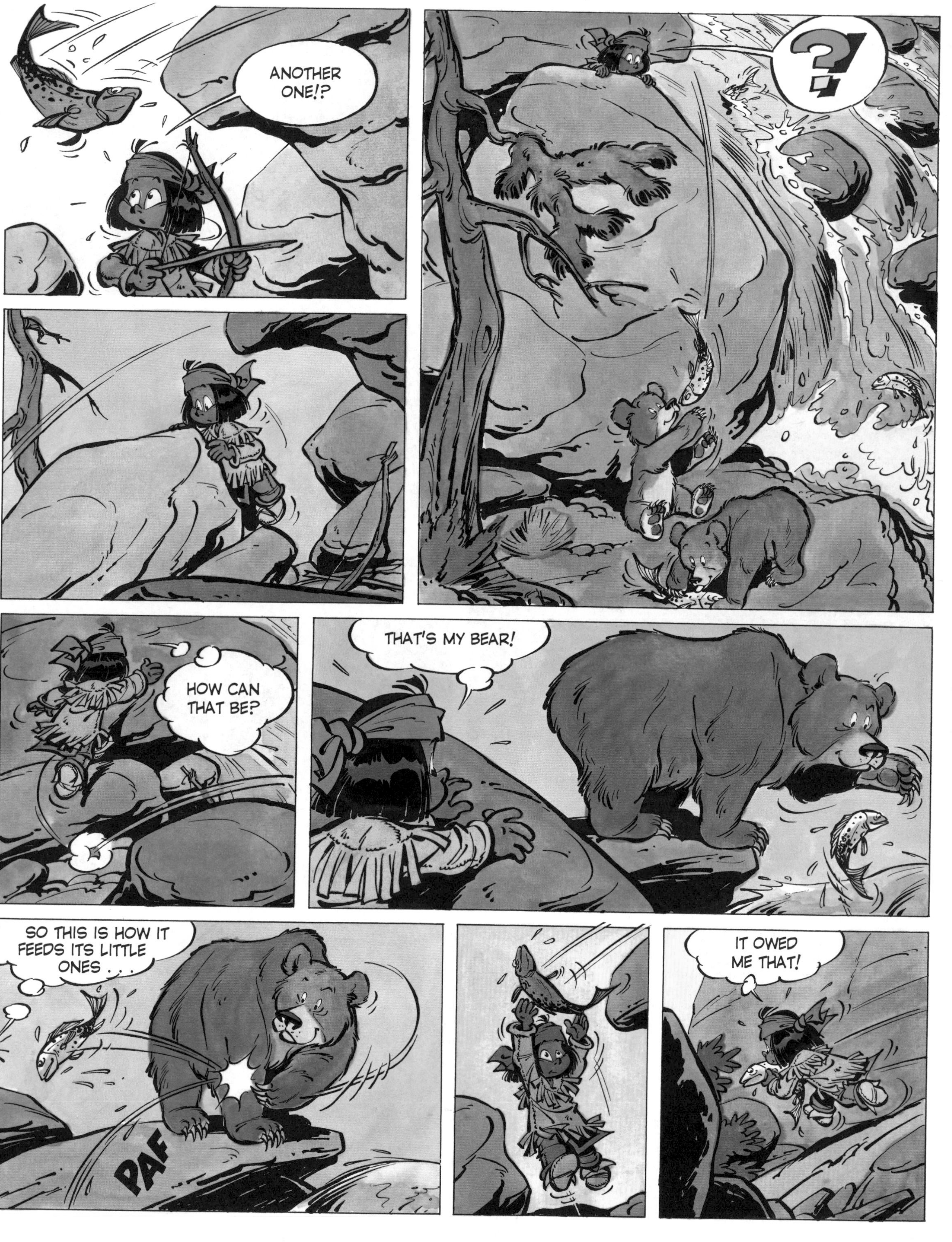
ANOTHER ONE!?
?!
HOW CAN THAT BE?
THAT'S MY BEAR!
SO THIS IS HOW IT FEEDS ITS LITTLE ONES . . .
PAF
IT OWED ME THAT!

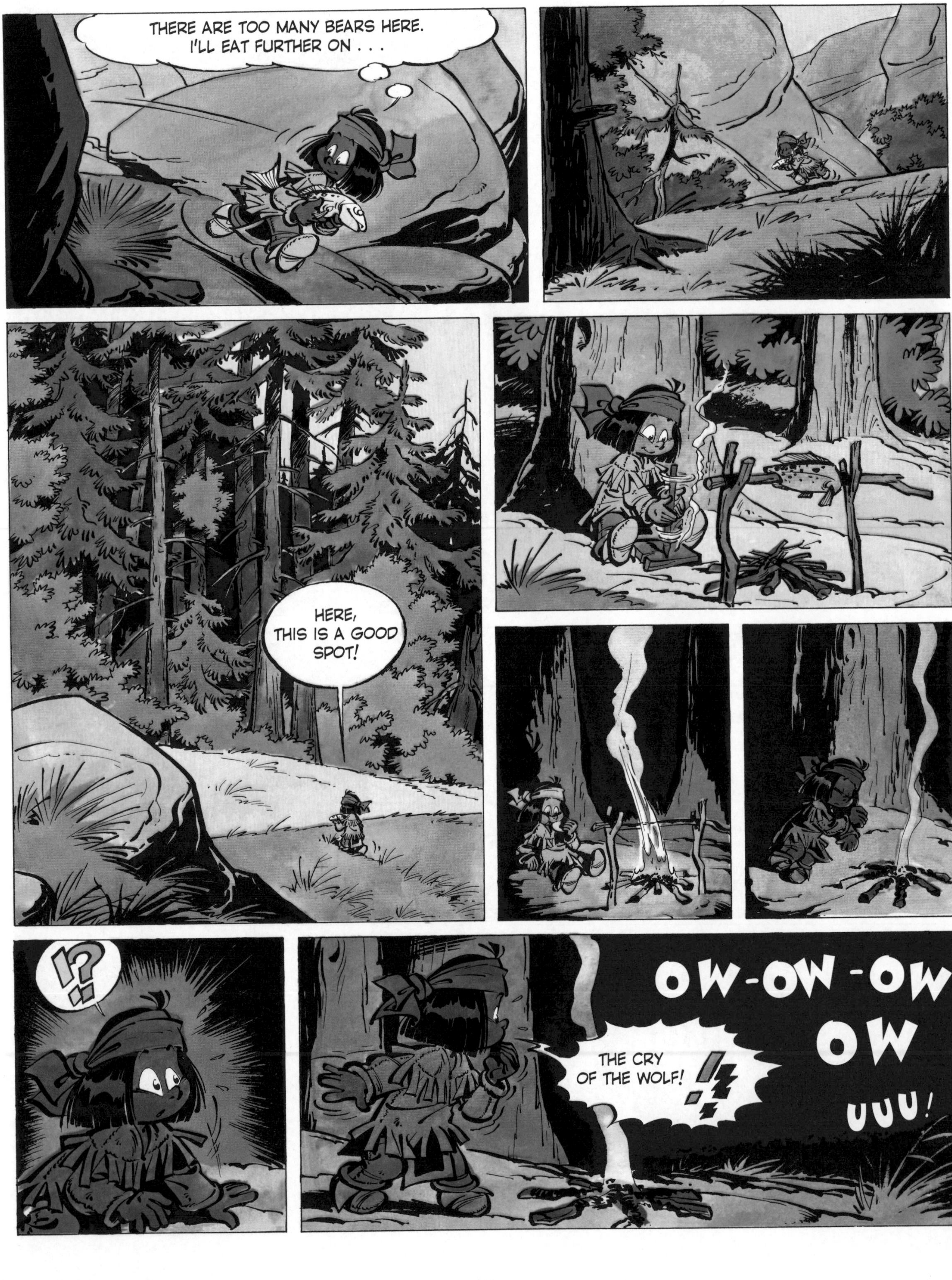

THERE ARE TOO MANY BEARS HERE. I'LL EAT FURTHER ON . . .
HERE, THIS IS A GOOD SPOT!
!?
THE CRY OF THE WOLF!
OW-OW-OW OW UUU!

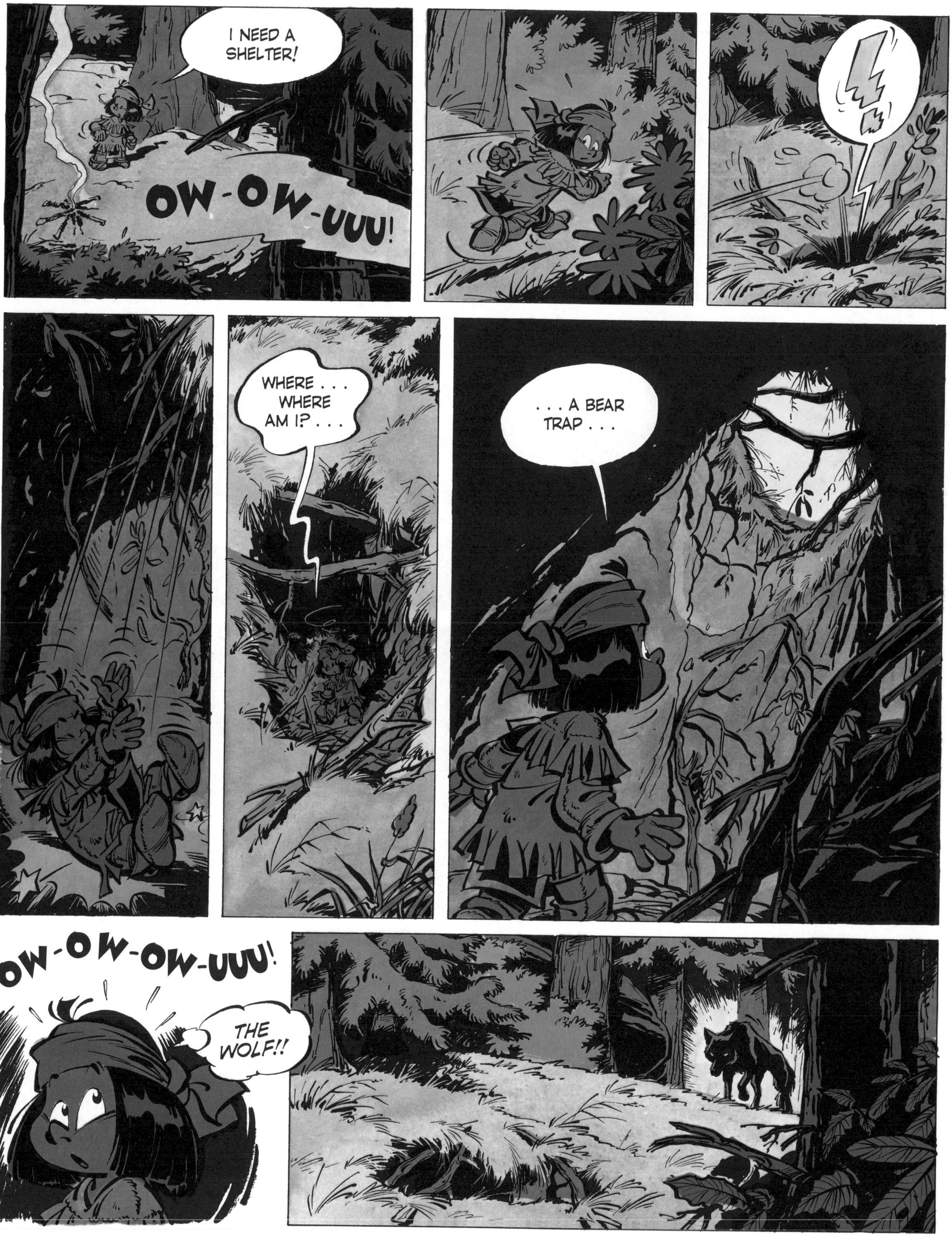
I NEED A SHELTER!
OW-OW-UUU!
WHERE . . . WHERE AM I? . . .
. . . A BEAR TRAP . . .
OW-OW-OW-UUU!
THE WOLF!!

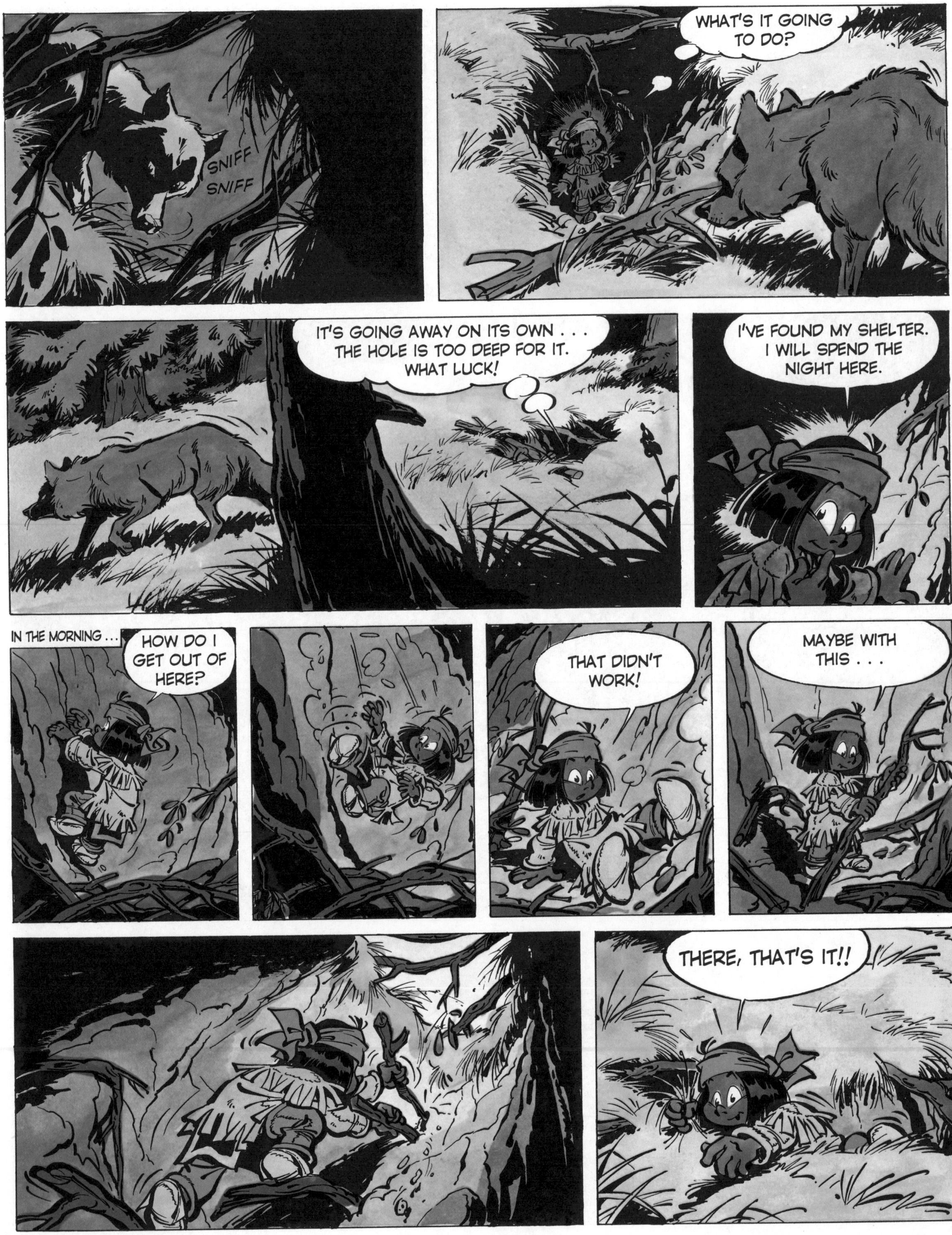
SNIFF
SNIFF
WHAT'S IT GOING TO DO?
IT'S GOING AWAY ON ITS OWN . . . THE HOLE IS TOO DEEP FOR IT. WHAT LUCK!
I'VE FOUND MY SHELTER. I WILL SPEND THE NIGHT HERE.
IN THE MORNING . . .
HOW DO I GET OUT OF HERE?
THAT DIDN'T WORK!
MAYBE WITH THIS . . .
THERE, THAT'S IT!!

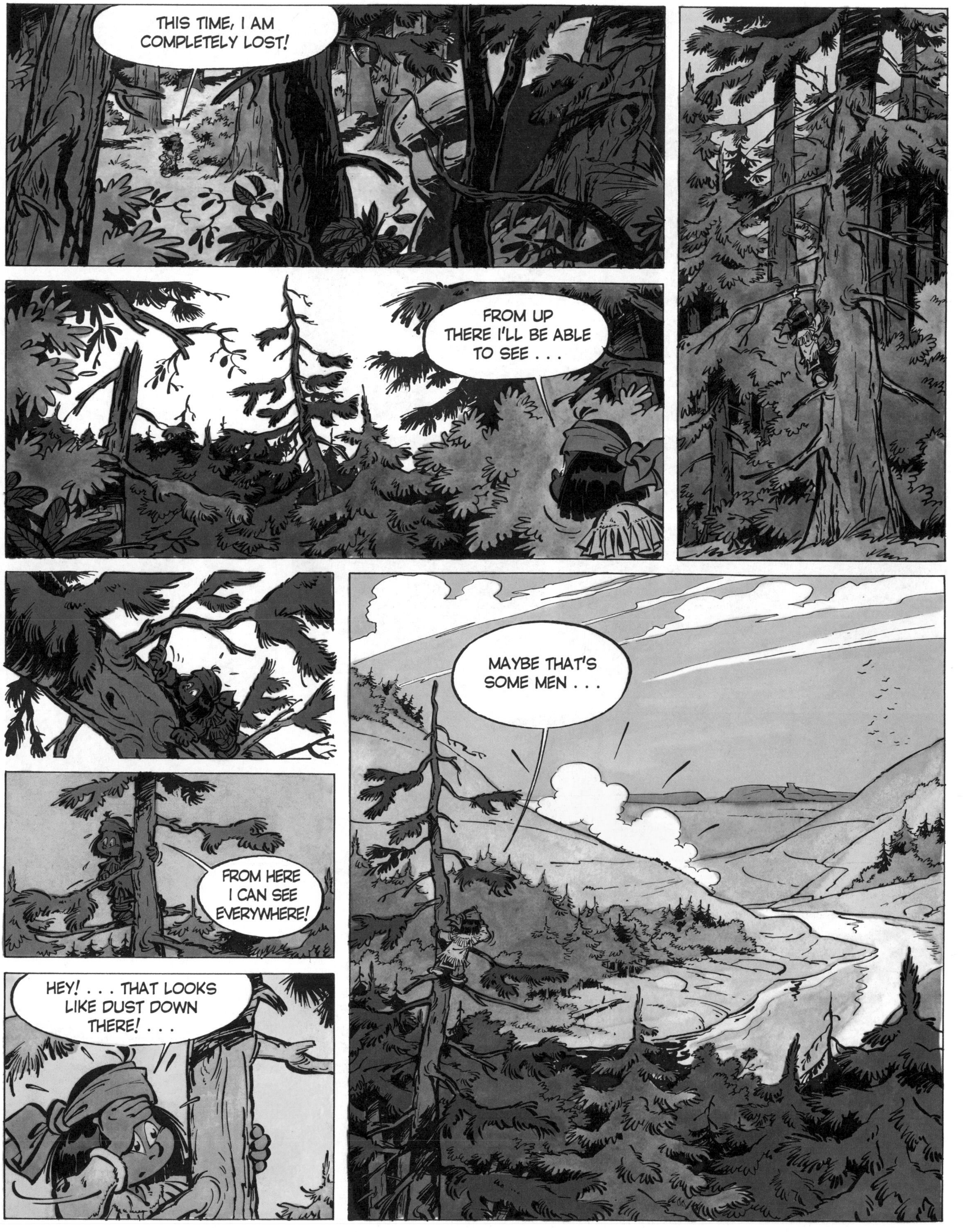
THIS TIME, I AM COMPLETELY LOST!
FROM UP THERE I'LL BE ABLE TO SEE . . .
FROM HERE I CAN SEE EVERYWHERE!
HEY! . . . THAT LOOKS LIKE DUST DOWN THERE! . . .
MAYBE THAT'S SOME MEN . . .

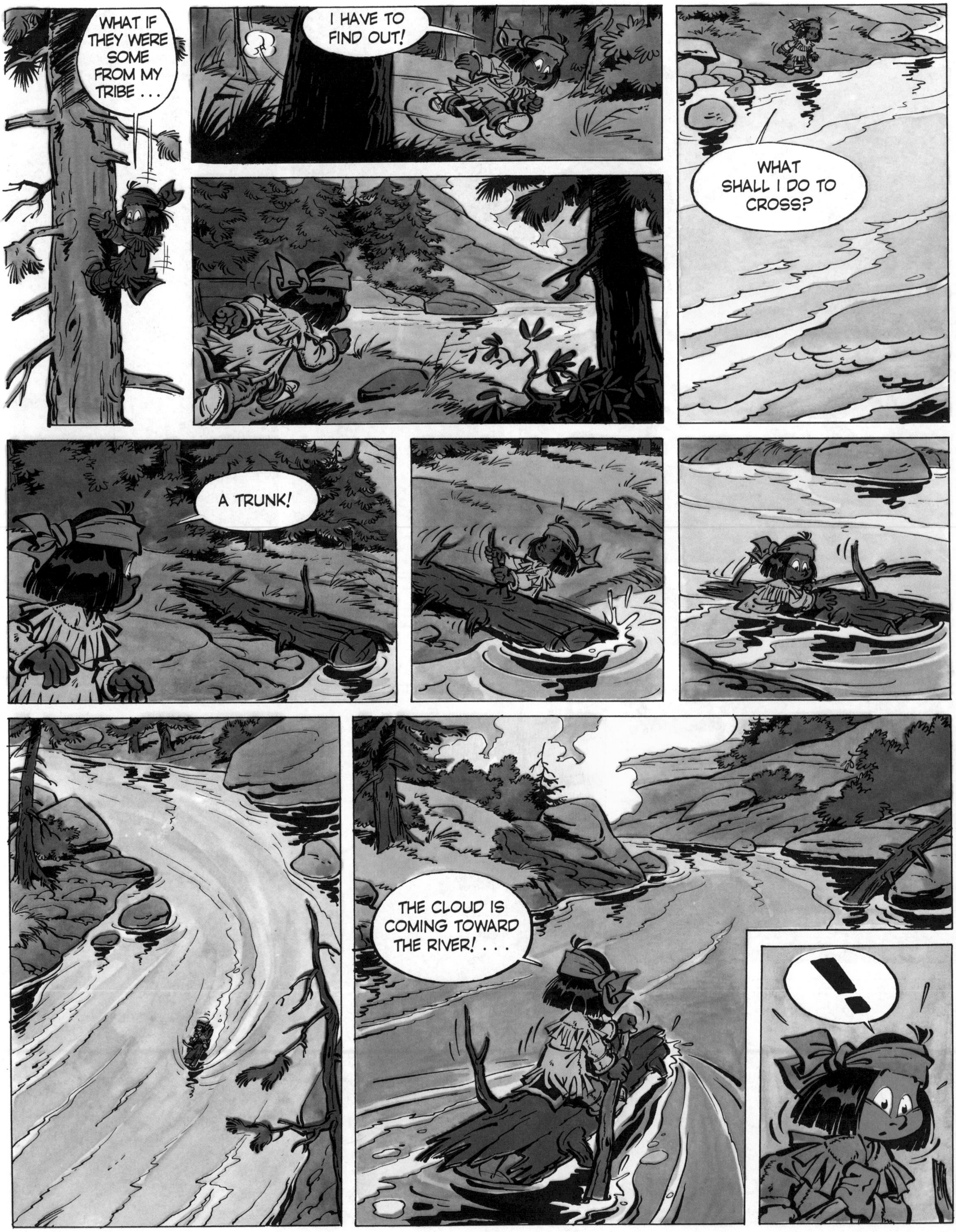
WHAT IF THEY WERE SOME FROM MY TRIBE . . .
I HAVE TO FIND OUT!
WHAT SHALL I DO TO CROSS?
A TRUNK!
THE CLOUD IS COMING TOWARD THE RIVER! . . .
!

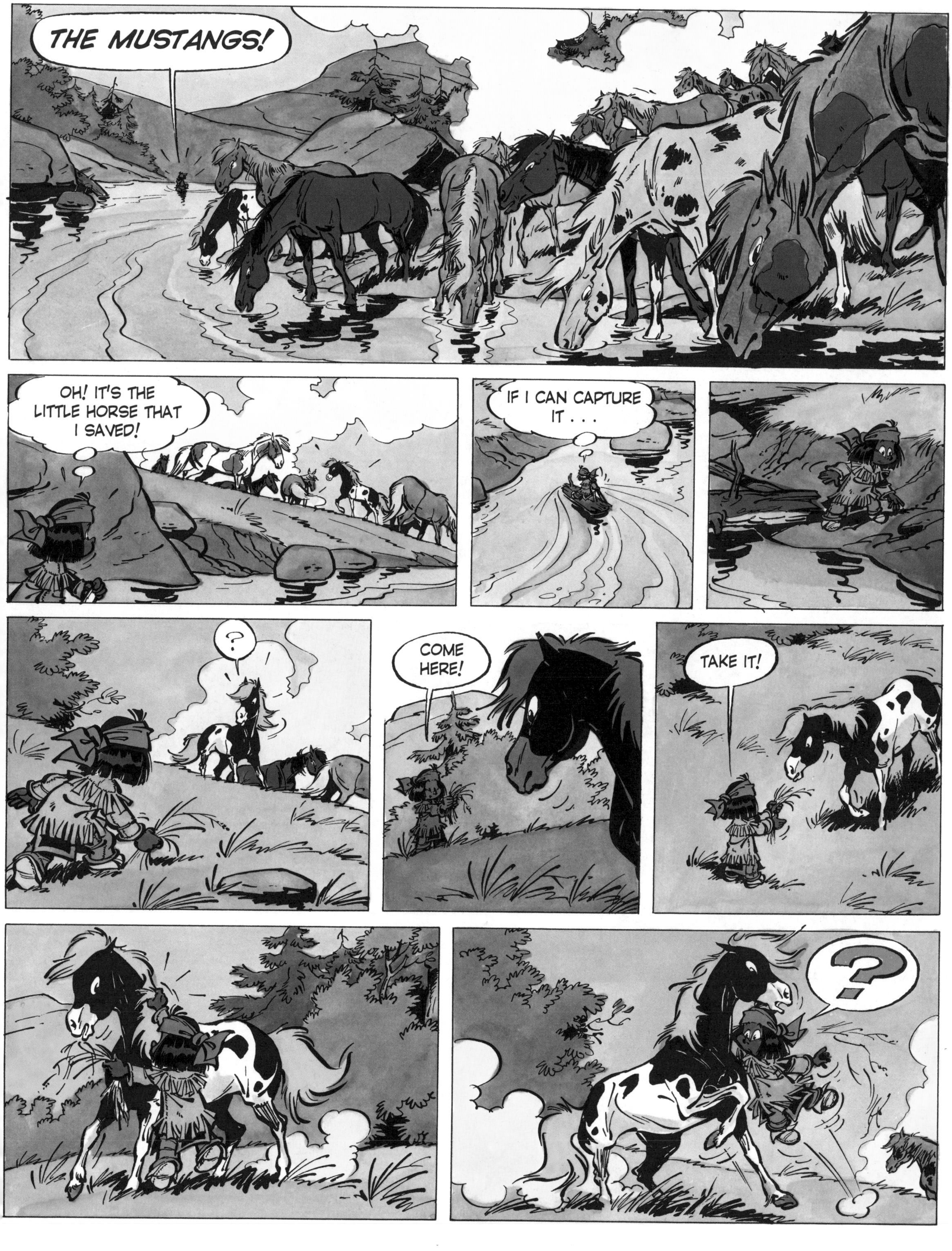
THE MUSTANGS!
OH! IT'S THE LITTLE HORSE THAT I SAVED!
IF I CAN CAPTURE IT . . .
?
COME HERE!
TAKE IT!
?

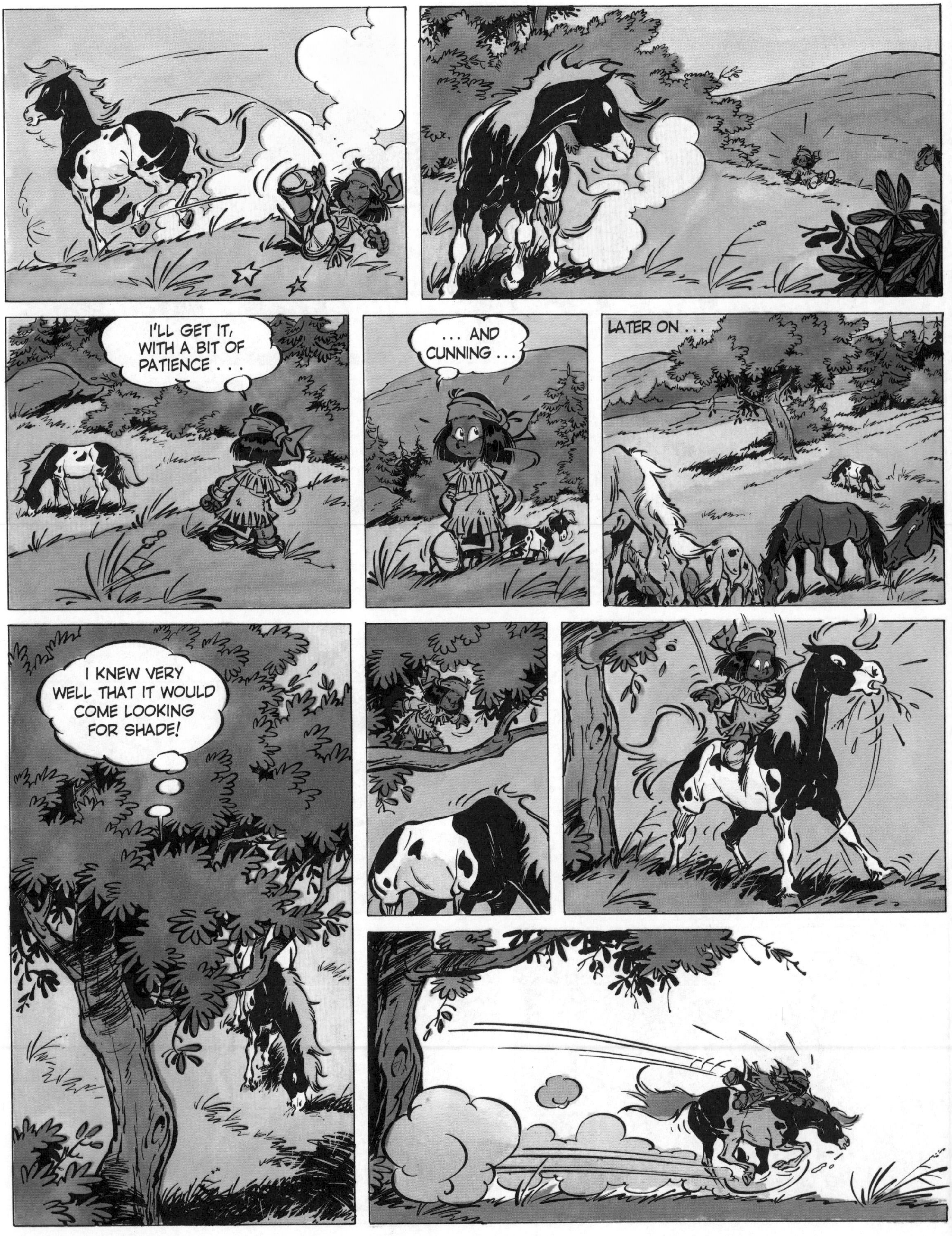
I'LL GET IT, WITH A BIT OF PATIENCE . . .
. . . AND CUNNING . . .
LATER ON . . .
I KNEW VERY WELL THAT IT WOULD COME LOOKING FOR SHADE!

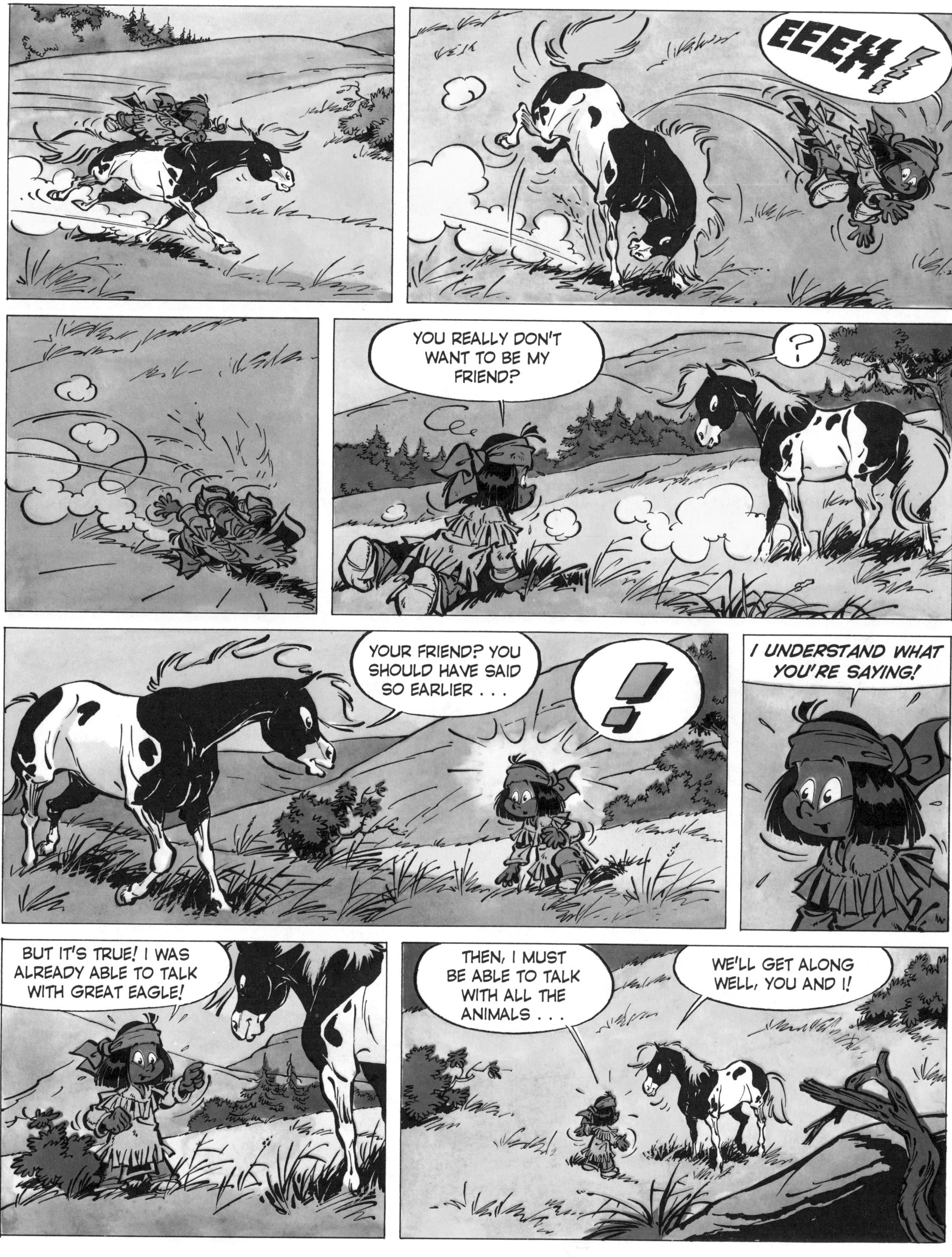
EEEK!
YOU REALLY DON'T WANT TO BE MY FRIEND?
?
YOUR FRIEND? YOU SHOULD HAVE SAID SO EARLIER . . .
!
I UNDERSTAND WHAT YOU'RE SAYING!
BUT IT'S TRUE! I WAS ALREADY ABLE TO TALK WITH GREAT EAGLE!
THEN, I MUST BE ABLE TO TALK WITH ALL THE ANIMALS . . .
WE'LL GET ALONG WELL, YOU AND I!

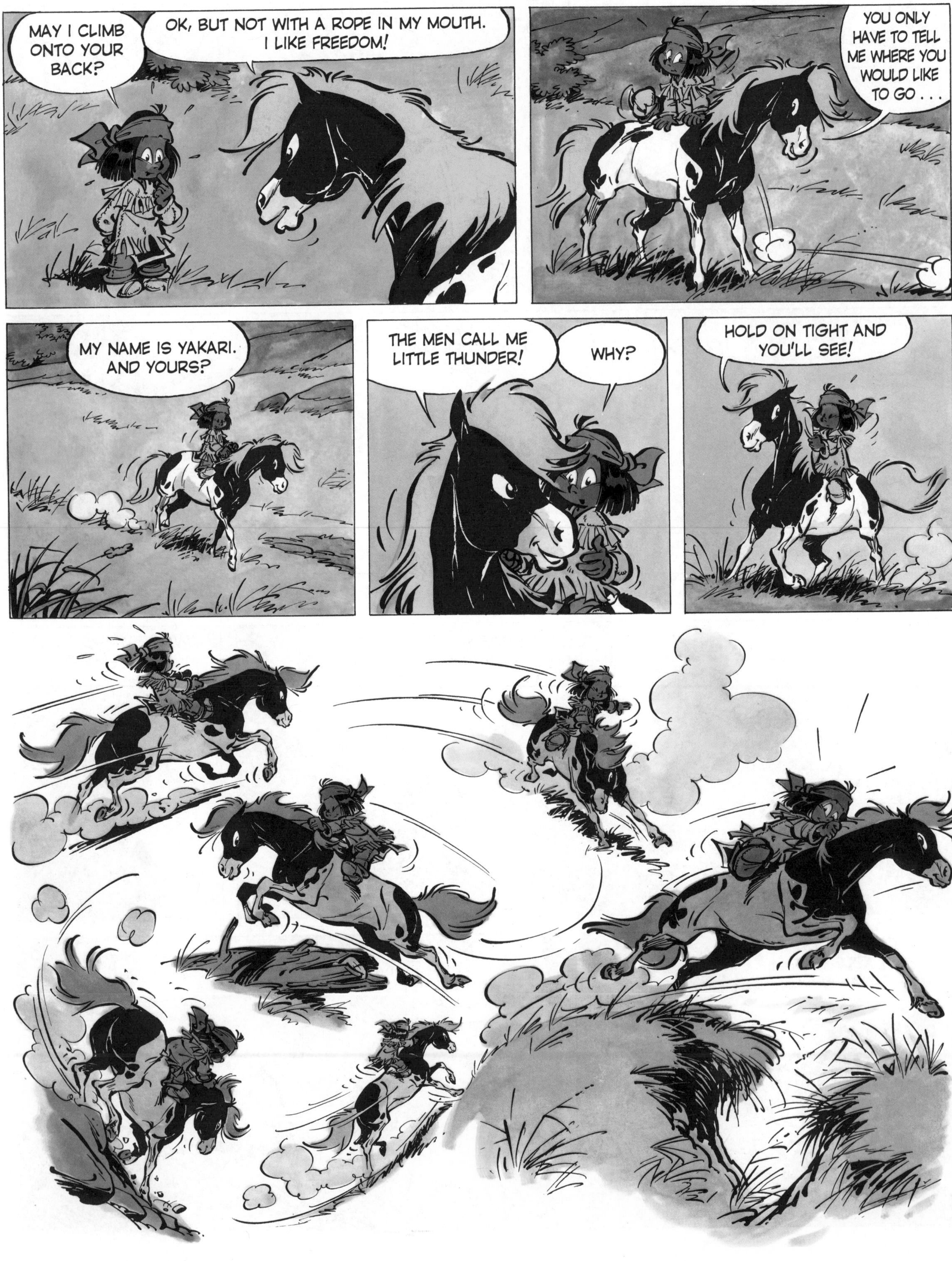

MAY I CLIMB ONTO YOUR BACK?
OK, BUT NOT WITH A ROPE IN MY MOUTH. I LIKE FREEDOM!
YOU ONLY HAVE TO TELL ME WHERE YOU WOULD LIKE TO GO . . .
MY NAME IS YAKARI. AND YOURS?
THE MEN CALL ME LITTLE THUNDER!
WHY?
HOLD ON TIGHT AND YOU'LL SEE!

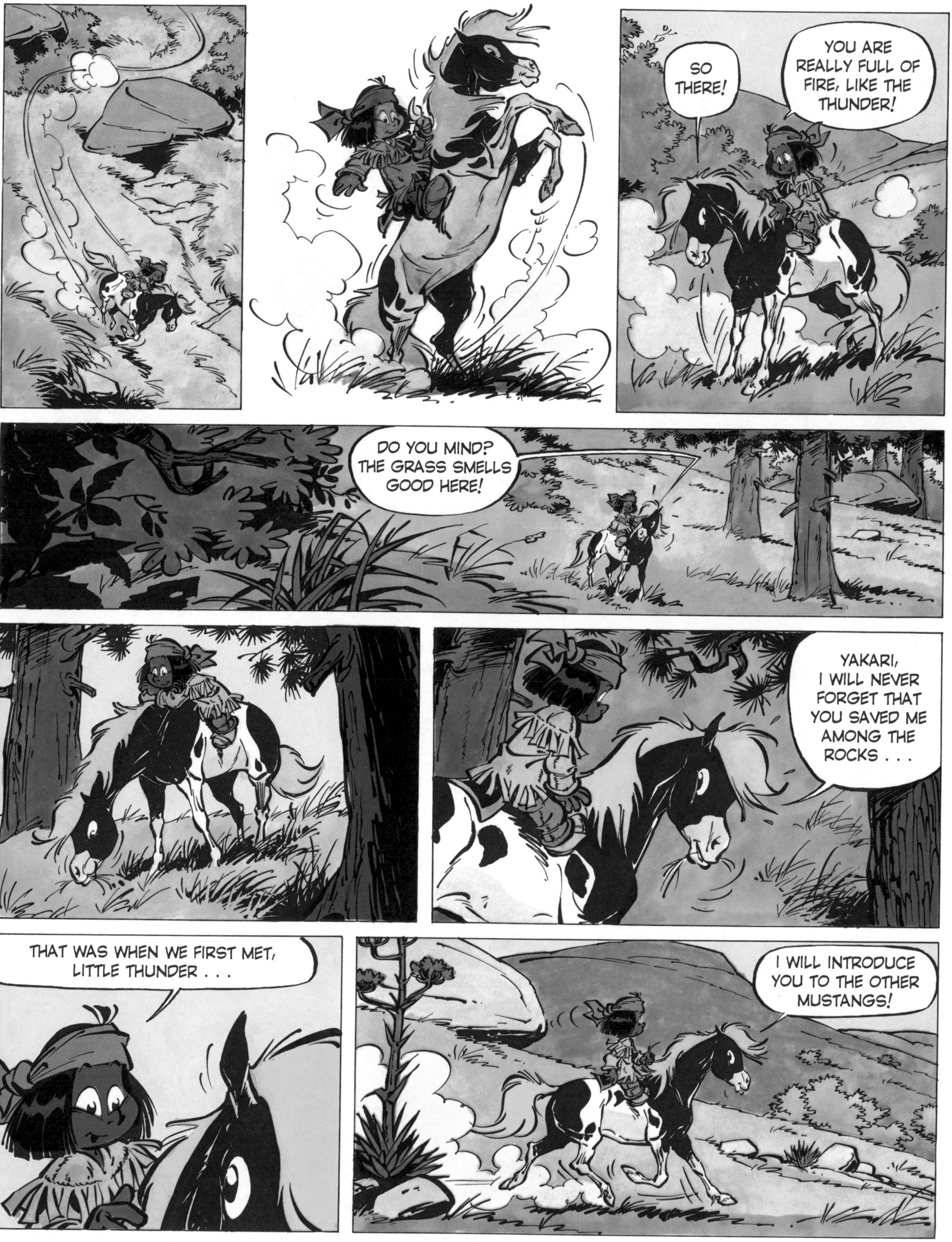

SO THERE!
YOU ARE REALLY FULL OF FIRE, LIKE THE THUNDER!
DO YOU MIND? THE GRASS SMELLS GOOD HERE!
YAKARI, I WILL NEVER FORGET THAT YOU SAVED ME AMONG THE ROCKS . . .
THAT WAS WHEN WE FIRST MET, LITTLE THUNDER . . .
I WILL INTRODUCE YOU TO THE OTHER MUSTANGS!

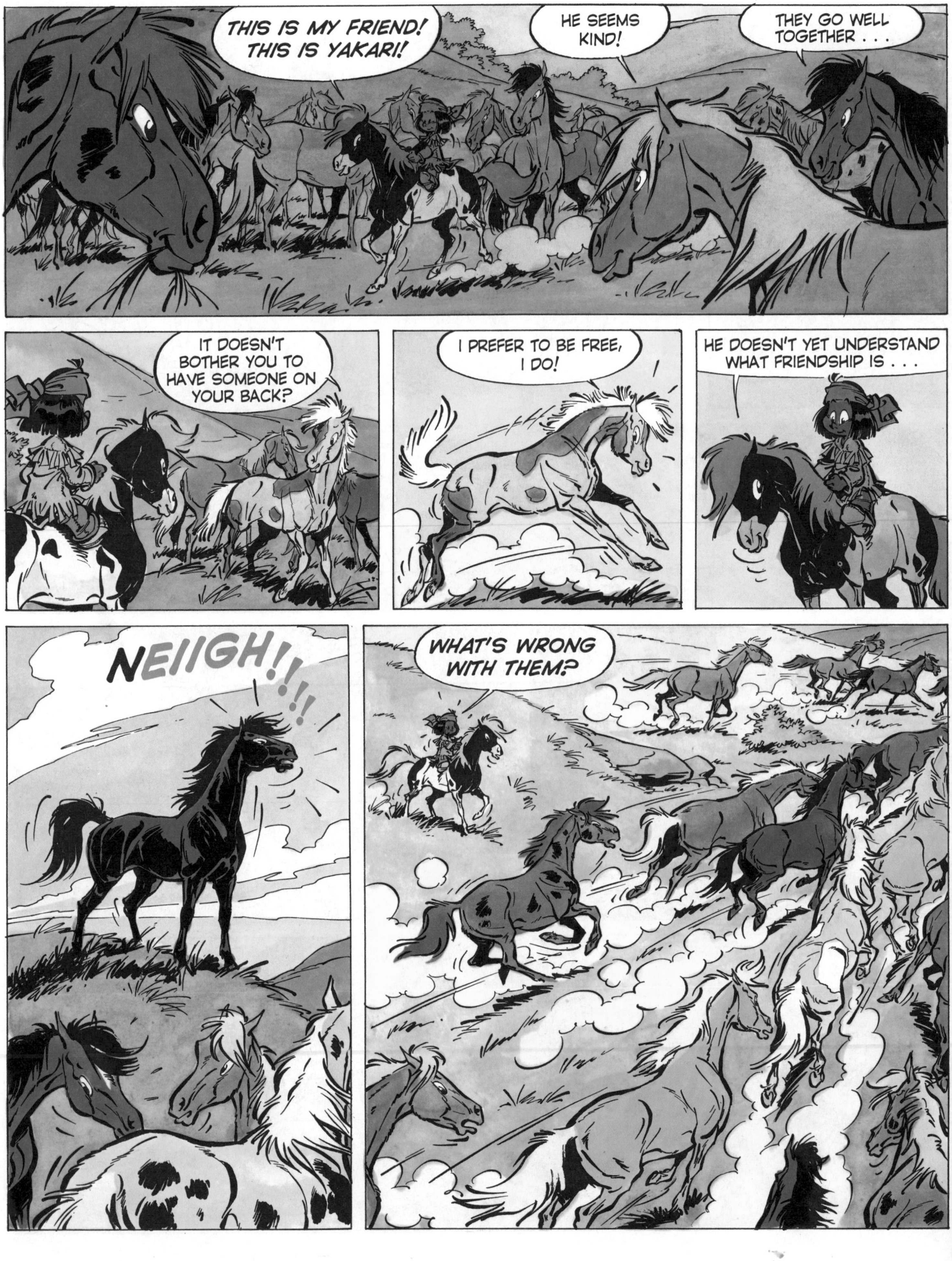
THIS IS MY FRIEND! THIS IS YAKARI!
HE SEEMS KIND!
THEY GO WELL TOGETHER . . .
IT DOESN'T BOTHER YOU TO HAVE SOMEONE ON YOUR BACK?
I PREFER TO BE FREE, I DO!
HE DOESN'T YET UNDERSTAND WHAT FRIENDSHIP IS . . .
NEIIGH!!!!
WHAT'S WRONG WITH THEM?

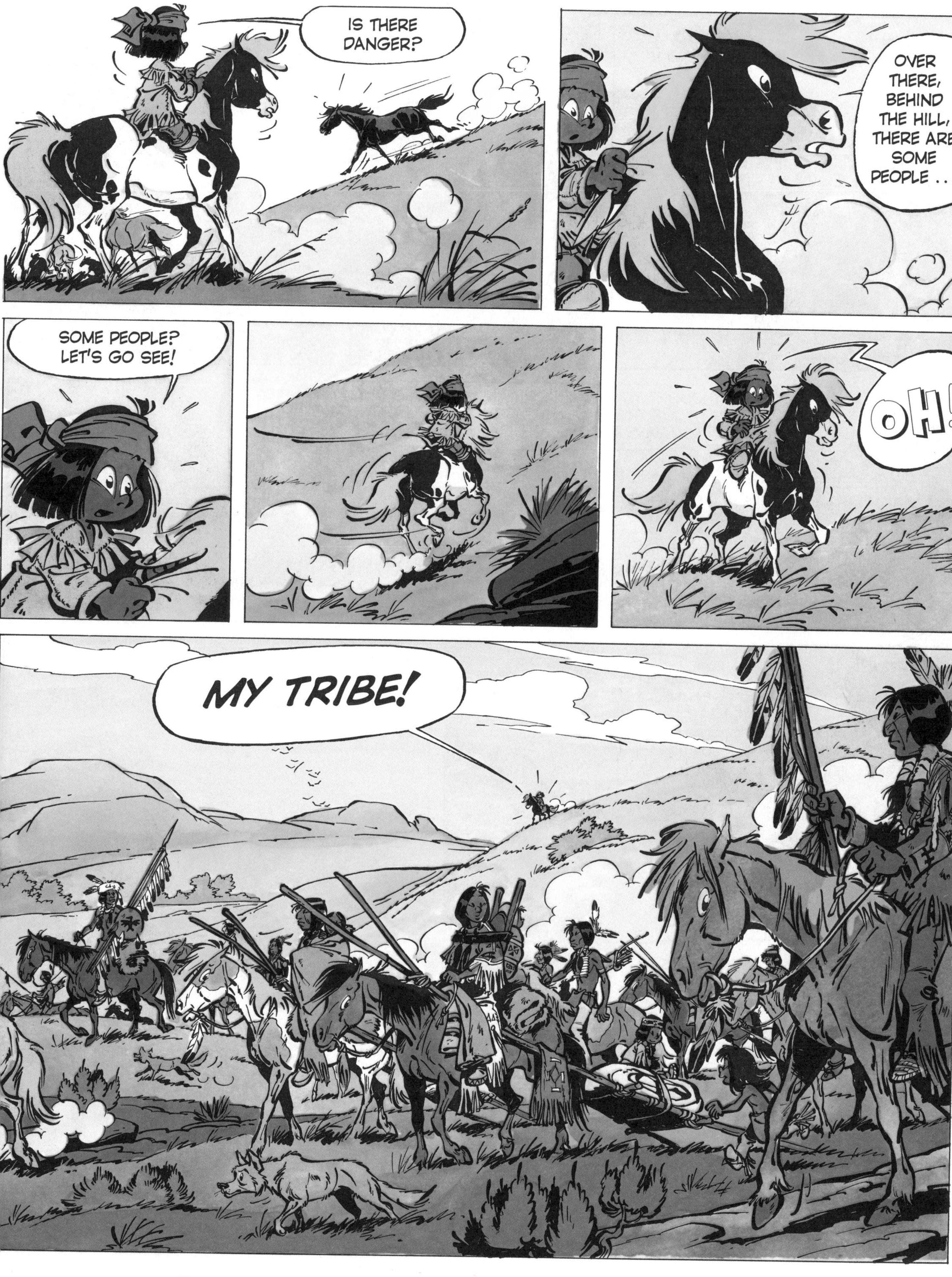
IS THERE DANGER?
OVER THERE, BEHIND THE HILL, THERE ARE SOME PEOPLE . . .
SOME PEOPLE? LET'S GO SEE!
OH!
MY TRIBE!

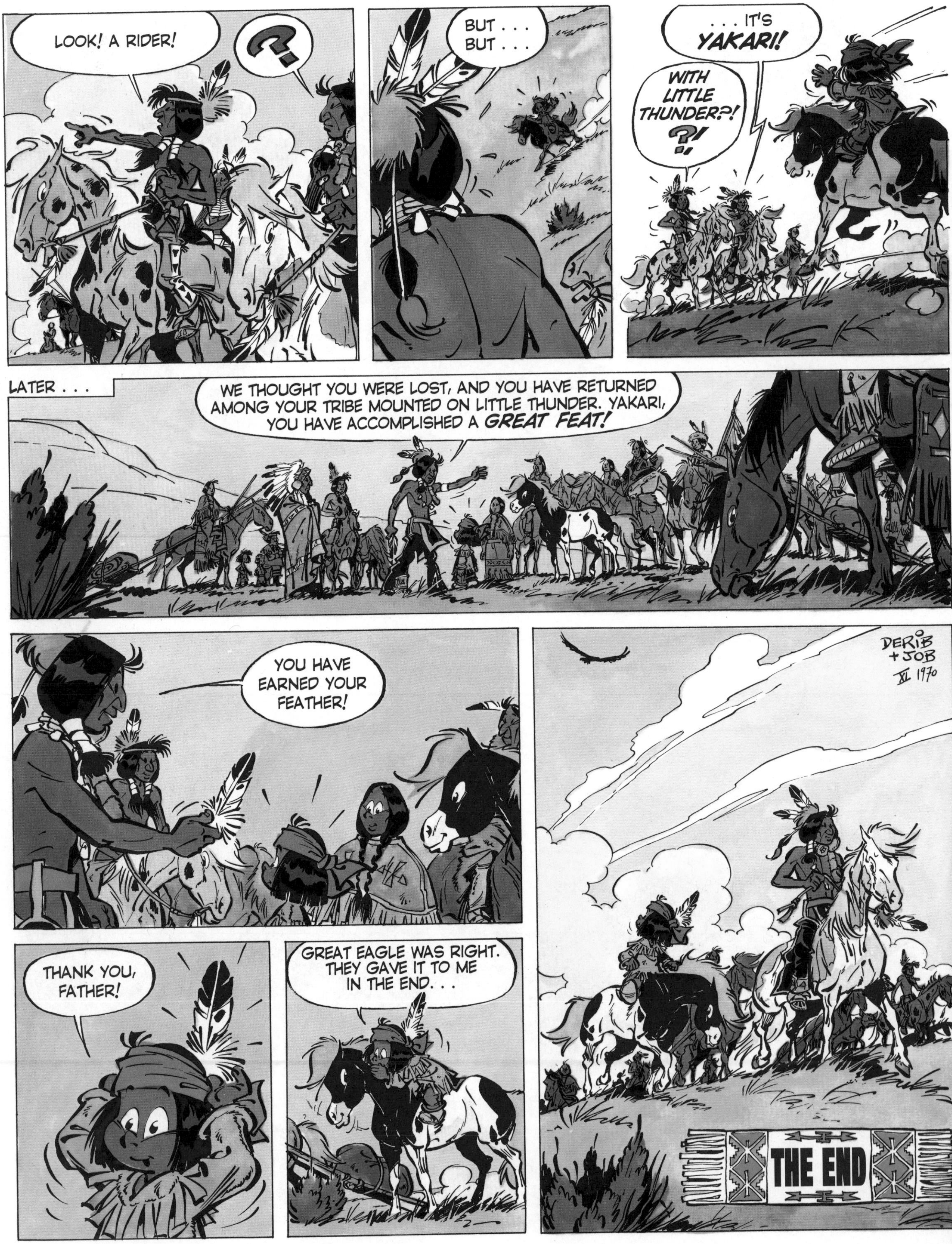
LOOK! A RIDER!
?
BUT . . .
BUT . . .
. . . IT'S YAKARI!
WITH LITTLE THUNDER?!
?!
LATER . . .
WE THOUGHT YOU WERE LOST, AND YOU HAVE RETURNED AMONG YOUR TRIBE MOUNTED ON LITTLE THUNDER. YAKARI, YOU HAVE ACCOMPLISHED A GREAT FEAT!
YOU HAVE EARNED YOUR FEATHER!
DERIB + JOB XI 1970
THANK YOU, FATHER!
GREAT EAGLE WAS RIGHT. THEY GAVE IT TO ME IN THE END. . .
THE END

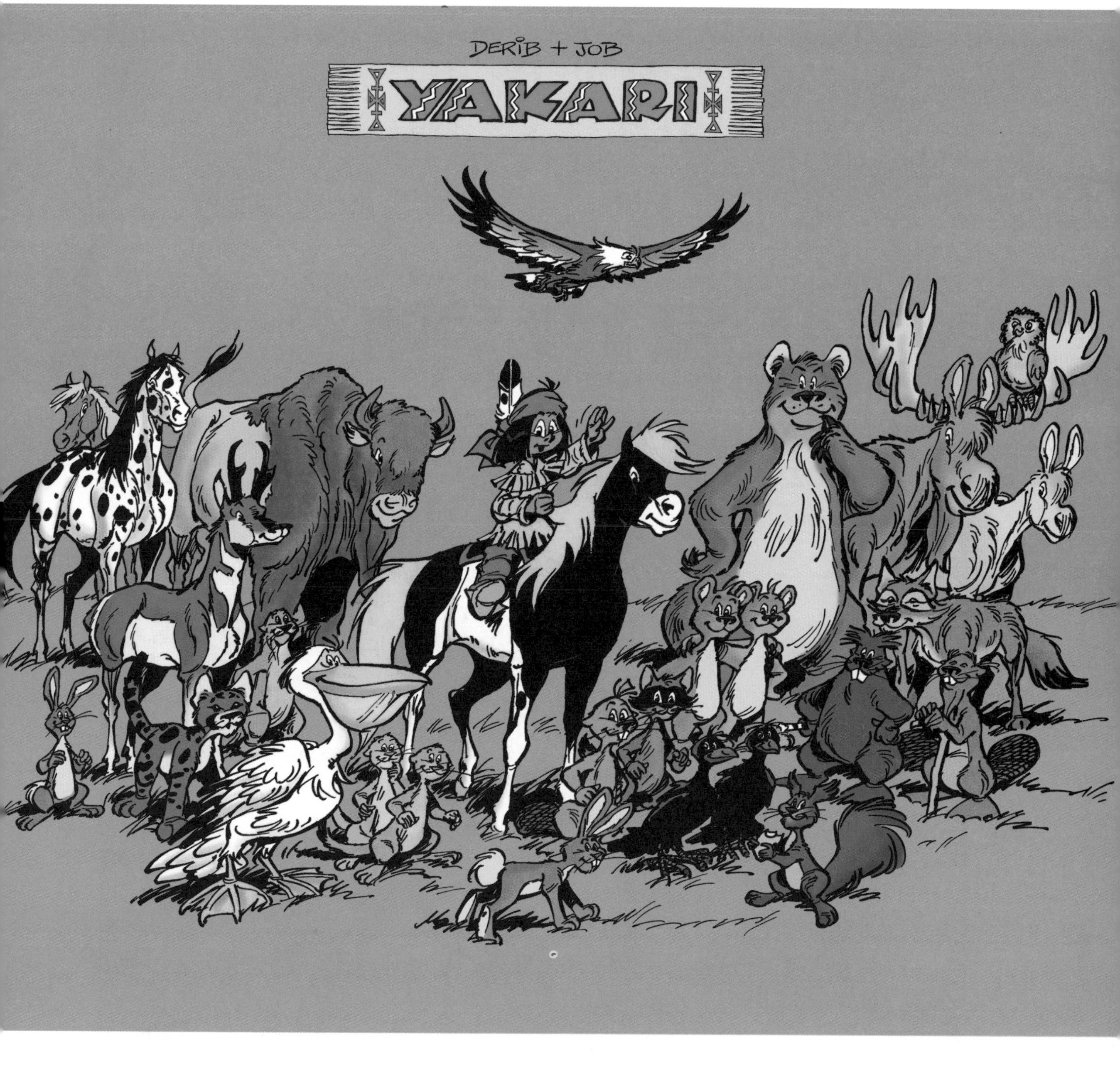
DERIB + JOB
YAKARI

SEE YOU SOON

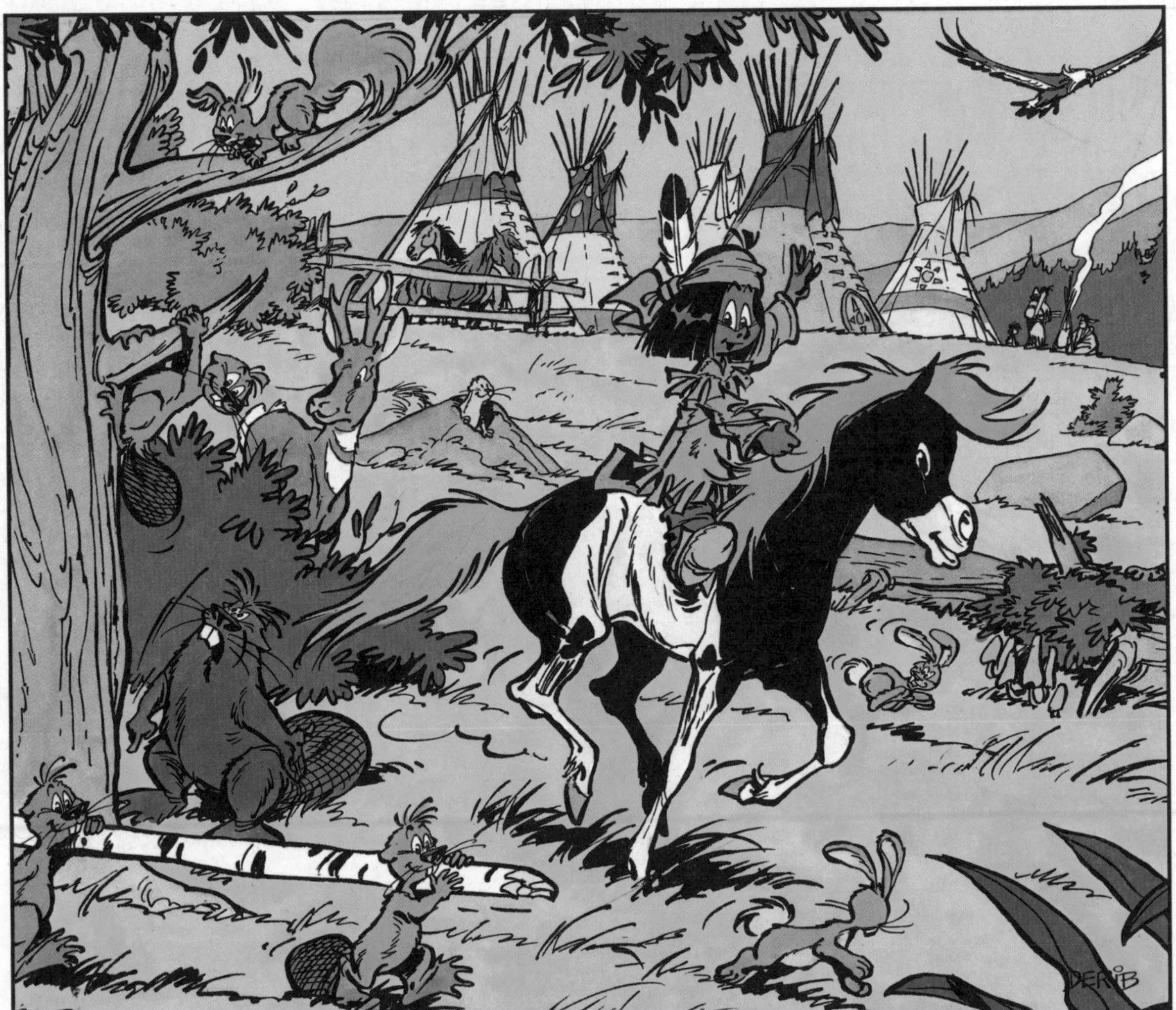
DERIB